WE'RE ON OUR WAY TO FRANCE!

How did tiny Castle Albion ever get into the UEFA Cup? Read all about their unbelievable FA Cup run in Haydn Middleton's first fantastic series:

1. COME AND HAVE A GO IF YOU THINK YOU'RE **SMART** ENOUGH!

2. COME AND HAVE A GO IF YOU THINK YOU'RE **COOL** ENOUGH!

3. COME AND HAVE A GO IF YOU THINK YOU'RE **MAD** ENOUGH!

4. COME AND HAVE A GO IF YOU THINK YOU'RE **RICH** ENOUGH!

And don't forget to look out for the further net-busting adventures of Luke Green, Cool Frederick, and all Benny Webb's Barmy Army:

1. WE'RE ON OUR WAY TO GERMANY!
2. WE'RE ON OUR WAY TO RUSSIA!
4. WE'RE ON OUR WAY TO ITALY!

WE'RE ON OUR WAY TO FRANCE!

Haydn Middleton

■ SCHOLASTIC

Scholastic Children's Books,
Commonwealth House, 1-19 New Oxford Street,
London, WC1A 1NU, UK
a division of Scholastic Ltd
London ~ New York ~ Toronto ~ Sydney ~ Auckland
Mexico City ~ New Delhi ~ Hong Kong

First published in the UK by Scholastic Ltd, 2000

Text copyright © Haydn Middleton, 2000

ISBN 0 439 01467 0

All rights reserved

Typeset by TW Typesetting, Midsomer Norton, Somerset
Printed and bound by The Bath Press, Bath

1 2 3 4 5 6 7 8 9 10

1

"Are we nearly there yet, Rodney?"

Luke tried to stretch in the old Ford Escort's passenger seat, but every part of him felt numb after three hours on the road. His stepdad Rodney shook his head helplessly. "It's always like this on the M25," he replied. "Bumper to bumper all the way round London. Even on a Wednesday afternoon in April. How are you doing in the back there, Frederick?"

"I'm cool," purred Luke's best mate, lounging across the back seat as he tapped out urgent e-mails on his laptop. Like Luke he was still at school, but in his spare time he made a small fortune from his own rare records search service – as well as coining it in as a red-hot rapper, not to mention his sky-high fees as a party DJ. He had already made more money out of music than Mozart ever did.

"It's good of you to come," Luke called back over the splutter and hiss of Rodney's dodgy stereo as the Escort crawled another few yards forward. "I need all the help I can get. Safety in numbers, you know? I'm just sorry it's taking so long." He looked at his watch. "The plane is going to be coming in any minute. We're not going to make it, are we, Rodney?"

"Oh, we will, we will," smiled Rodney, blinking behind his glasses. "Look, that sign says *Heathrow Airport 5 miles*. We ought to be there in no time now."

Rodney was always the optimist. Being married to Luke's mum, that came in very handy. Luke was so glad she'd had a headache and so hadn't come with them. She would have been No Fun At All in this traffic jam. Just thinking about that made Luke feel horribly wobbly. Which wasn't easy when you were already numb. And he *should* have been feeling in tip-top physical condition. Because tomorrow night little Luke Green – along with Cool Frederick Dulac there in the back – was going to play in the UEFA Cup semi-final (first leg)!

It still seemed like a dream to Luke. A dream that had begun just over a year before – when he proudly ran out as mascot for Nationwide League Division Three strugglers Castle Albion FC. Spotted by manager Benny Webb in the pre-match kick around, he was in the team before you could say Nicky Butt. A game or two later, Cool F was on board too. From there on in, it was pure storybook stuff.

Inspired by Luke and Frederick, Albion avoided almost certain relegation to the Football Conference. They weren't just concentrating on the league though. *As if!* Along the way, they also became the first-ever lower-division side to get to the FA Cup Final. Not only that: they won it – beating Man U three-one! Which put them into the hat for this year's UEFA Cup. And, although their league form was still a bit patchy, they'd gone from strength to strength in Europe.

After easing past Malta's Sliema Wanderers and Turkey's Fenerbahce, they were paired with mighty Bayern Munich of Germany. Two storming legs later they were through to the quarter-finals, where Russia's Spartak Moscow lay in wait. Was that the end of the road for Albion? Not on your Cossacks! After going down two-four at home they carved out a four-one away win to hit the semis.

Now all that lay between them and a place in the final in Rome's Olympic Stadium was super French side Paris Saint-Germain. Or PSG for short. And all that lay between Luke and a place in the Albion line-up tomorrow night was a PSP. Short for Pretty Scary Parent. In other words, Luke's dearest darling mum. Because she hated football even more than Dracula hated crosses. And if she ever found out about Luke's sideline as a soccer sensation, she would probably unscrew both of his feet at the ankles – just for starters.

"You really think it's going to be all right tomorrow?" Luke asked Rodney. "You'll be able to get mum safely out of town and everything? I mean, you've got the tickets, right? And mum's said she's *definitely* going to go?"

"Relax, Luke." Rod patted his knee. They were picking up speed now. At last they'd left the jampacked motorway and were zooming towards Heathrow's Terminal One – or as near to zooming as Rodney's Escort could manage. "Everything's going to be fine. Your mum wouldn't miss this show for the world. She practically *smiled* when I told her about it!"

"Hmmm," said Luke, frowning. Rod was planning to take his mad-keen gardener mum to Birmingham's NEC. To the official opening of the *Ideal Gnome Exhibition*. Luke's mum liked garden gnomes. Sure she did. But would she want to go all the way to Birmingham just to see a state-of-the-art selection of the things from around the world?

"There's no doubt at all that she'll come," Rodney said. "And you know what the clincher was? I told her that a certain *celebrity* might be there." He winked. "A smoothie TV star with a *grey moustache* who does *gardening* adverts?"

"Des Lynam!" gasped Luke. "But he won't be at any gnome exhibition! He'll be presenting Albion v PSG live on ITV!"

Rodney tapped his nose with one finger. "*I*

know that. *You* know that. But your mum –
bless her – doesn't know that. And I think she'd
go a lot further than Birmingham if she thought
she was going to get a glimpse of Des in the
flesh."

Luke stared through the windscreen at the
terminal up ahead. Rodney was right enough
about his mum's obsession with Laid-Back
Lynam. She lapped him up so much, she even
ignored the awful fact that he'd first found fame
as a *football* presenter. Some evenings she sat
glued to the TV for six hours at a stretch, just in
the hope of catching one of his gardening ads.
If she could have grown a moustache herself,
as a mark of respect, she'd have done it. Luke
could only hope Rodney's plan would work,
leaving *him* free to play. (Even so, he didn't
fancy being in his stepdad's shoes when she
found out that the NEC was a Des-Free Zone.)

"Look, you lads," panted Rodney, jerking to a
halt outside the terminal but not switching off
the engine, "I'll have to drop you here then go
and park. The plane's already in. We can't let
her arrive and find nobody waiting."

"No sweat," agreed Cool F, snapping shut his
laptop and tapping Luke on the shoulder. "Let's
go find the lady!"

Luke pulled a face as he opened the car door
and got out. *Women!* Whichever way he
turned, he had woman-trouble. If it wasn't his

football-hating mum, it was the football-*loving* young lady he was about to meet off the plane.

A girl called Uschi, with a crush on Luke as big as Luke's mum's on Des.

2

"Hey, stop trembling, man," Fred said in Luke's ear. "She'll think you're all wound up about seeing her again. She'll think it's a ... *lurve thang*!"

Luke snorted (but still went on trembling). A love thing? He thought not! There was nothing *wrong* with Uschi. It was just that she was big. Really big. All over. *Crushingly* big – as Albion's whizzkid player-chairman-owner James "Jimbo" Prince had found, shortly before the UEFA tie in Munich.

Just outside the dressing-room, Uschi had tripped up and taken a tumble right on top of the lad who had made his millions in computer games. That had put him out of the tie before a ball was kicked. Which won her the undying gratitude of everyone else connected with Castle Albion. Because Jimbo, who insisted on playing for the club he had saved from extinction last May, was quite possibly the world's worst footballer over the age of four. (And there were quite a few two- and three-year-olds who had the edge over him too.) Sadly for Albion, though, he was fit and well and raring to go against PSG.

"Oh, why did she choose *this* week to come over?" Luke asked under his breath.

"Luck of the draw?" suggested Frederick. "Hey, she had to come *sometime*."

That was true enough. Uschi was Luke's German Exchange partner. He'd spent a few days at her home in Munich. Now she had to come and stay with him. That's the way these things worked. The school arranged them all the time. But in Luke's case the arrangement had been a bit special. A *very* last-minute thing. His headmistress had fixed it all up with Uschi's family, who were big mates of hers. Why? Because the head was a lifelong Albion fan, and she wanted to make sure Luke got to play in the away leg against Bayern.

"Is *that* her?" cried Luke, pointing over the heads of the people waiting in front.

"Keep it real." Cool F shook his head, just once. "That's a baggage-trolley."

And it was – a jumbo-sized one too, stacked up to overflowing. But to be fair to Luke, it was a wonder he could see anything at all. Like Frederick, he was wearing dark glasses, with a baseball cap pulled way down in front. But Frederick dressed like that most of the time anyway. For Luke it was a vital disguise.

Most places they went, both boys got mobbed by starstruck footie fans. Thanks to TV coverage of their Cup heroics they were household names all over the country (except, of course, in Luke's own household). And their agent Neil Veal had milked that by getting them a host of sponsorship deals. On their way into the terminal they'd passed a massive poster of Cool F advertising his Adidas *Fredator* boots. Near it was another one for a new-flavour glucose drink called *Luke-o-zade*. It only showed Luke from behind, swigging from a bottle – in case his mum ever caught sight of it – but now that his rear-view had become so well-known too, he had to wear a hunchback's hump under his fleece, just so he didn't get spotted.

But in spite of all that, a hand came down on his shoulder and Luke heard the dreaded words in a hoarse whisper: "Well, well! What have we here? Mr Studless, I believe!" (One of Luke's nicknames was "Studless Sensation" – he still played in trainers because his mum had never let him have any football boots when he was smaller, and now he just couldn't get used to them.)

Luke swivelled around expecting to find someone thrusting an autograph book under his nose. Instead he found an equally weird-looking guy grinning at him. The hair on top of his head was jet black and beautifully shaped in a classic Elvis-Presley style. The hair on his chin was vintage Jimmy Hill. Both were entirely artificial – because, as Luke saw at once, beneath the wigs was Albion's left midfielder Chrissie "Bald Bombshell" Pick!

"What's happenin'?" asked Frederick, high-fiving him lightning fast before they drew anyone's attention. Chrissie was almost as big a magnet for mobbing as the two schoolboys. He wasn't that much older than them. In fact he'd come to Albion as a YTS trainee only a couple of years before. Another client of Neil Veal's, he'd done a few fashion shows for Armani and Versace. He didn't look too good in the photos – especially in a blue-and-white hooped sarong – but that hadn't stopped a stream of super-models from going all soppy over him.

"I'm here to meet a girl from Zurich," Chrissie sighed, keeping his voice as low as the brim of Luke's cap. "She's been phoning me all week begging for a ticket for tomorrow. But I don't think she really likes football at all. None of them do. They can't even remember the score afterwards."

"It's you they're after, man," Frederick told him. "Respect to the sexy slaphead *in* the airport."

"Yeah? Well, I'm getting fed up with it," said Chrissie. "I just want someone that I can take to the chip shop and listen to my Prodigy tapes with."

"I don't think you'll be doing that with *her*," smiled Luke, nodding over at the Arrivals area. Everyone else was looking that way too, their eyes out on stalks. A cat-suited vision was cat-walking into view.

"Oh, flip me," groaned Chrissie as her cats-eyes picked him out and her whole fantastic face lit up. "Here we go again. I'll catch you lads later."

As he trudged off to say hello to his Swiss stunner, Luke took a long look round the great hall. "I reckon Uschi's been and gone," he murmured to Frederick.

His mate tilted his head slightly. Something had caught his attention over by the doors they had come in through. Luke looked too – and spotted Rodney, who was coming in after parking the car. But then he looked again. That was after he heard a chilling blast of "Luuuke! *Luuuuke!*"

A high-pitched, female blast. A blast erupting from a very great height. A blast that was all wrapped up in a blue-and-white bobble-hat, blue-and-white scarf and blue-and-white self-knitted Jacket. It was Uschi!

"Luuuke! *There* you are! Luuuuke! Oh *Luuukey!*" She broke into a trot.

Just at that moment Rodney caught sight of Luke too. Raising a hand, he quickened his stride towards his stepson. He never saw Uschi coming. She never saw him.

"No! *No!*" Luke yelled – too late. Uschi smacked into his stepdad with all the force of one of Roy Keane's tastiest tackles. Then Rodney's glasses were flying off his face and high up into the air...

3

Rodney didn't die. Not quite. It took a couple of airport security men to bring him round. Then he thought he'd gone blind from the impact. But when Frederick gave him back his glasses – which he'd dived forward and caught before they hit the deck – he started to get everything back into perspective.

Luke and Cool F took him over to one of the cafés, sat him down, and bought him three coffees. Slowly but surely, that brought him right back round. Uschi, meanwhile, sat on her stack of suitcases a little way back from the table.

She'd been terribly apologetic about clattering Rodney. But now she was deadly quiet. To begin with, Luke thought she was just too embarrassed by the whole incident to talk. On the other hand, this wasn't the first time she'd flattened a bloke. First Jimbo, now Rodney. Maybe it was regular thing with her.

And she certainly didn't *look* embarrassed

any more. As Luke got Rodney to drink up his coffees, he kept snatching glances at her. Each time, her eyes met his full-on. And she had this faint but unmistakable smile. Luke quickly smiled back but something about that look in her eyes worried him. Sort of dreamy, yet piercing as well. It was as if she was trying to say something to him. Something important. Something, no doubt, to do with her and him.

"So are you looking forward to the game tomorrow, then, Uschi?" Rodney asked her, reaching for his third coffee. "Luke tells me you're a big Albion fan."

"*Ja*, that is so," she said in her surprisingly small voice. "My team is Castle Albion." She turned that weird look on Luke again. "But I believe that I would support *any* team for which Lukey played."

Luke went red. As red as he'd gone in Munich when he'd seen Uschi's bedroom walls. They had been smothered in photos of him – snipped from magazines, matchday programmes, news-papers, you name it. And then there had been a whole lot more pics. Ones that she'd drawn *herself* and coloured in.

"Respect to the midfield maestro," nodded Cool F, touching his fist to Luke's – and probably raising an eyebrow behind his shades. Luke was gladder than ever that Frederick was here with him to share the load.

"But you are a very fine player too," Uschi told Frederick. "Both defensively and also when you go on to the offensive. As a sweeper, you have no equal."

"Cheers," nodded Cool F. But already Uschi's eyes were back on Luke, and another uncomfortable silence followed.

"Well," said Rodney, breaking it, "we can only hope Albion have got their *Cup* hats on tomorrow night. In the league, things haven't been going too well."

"You can say that again," sighed Luke. "We're second from bottom, and we haven't won a league game since before the UEFA Cup tie in Moscow."

"Four nil-nil draws in a row," Rodney added. "We can keep the opposition out, thanks mainly to Frederick here. But we just can't get the ball in the net."

At that, Uschi frowned. "This puzzles me," she said. "When you came to play against Munich, you had the phenomenal Dogan Mezir up front. I have never seen a goalscorer of such class. He tore the Bayern defence to shreds. Surely *he* must be able to penetrate Nationwide League Division Three defences."

Luke, Frederick and Rodney all looked at one another and took a long, deep breath. "Ah now," sighed Rodney, getting ready to fill her in. "The Dog. Now that's a *real* mystery..."

Indeed it was. Superstriker Dogan Mezir, Albion's only new signing that season, had so far played in just *two* matches for the club: the away leg against Bayern, and the away leg in Moscow. He came from Armenia, where he'd been a sheepfarmer as well as a footballer. For months after his transfer to Albion, all kinds of family problems had kept him in his home country. But then an even bigger problem reared its head. Big burly Dog was utterly terrified of travelling on any form of powered transport.

Trains, cars, planes, ships – he'd never been on one in his life. He'd never, in fact, travelled more than twenty miles from his home village. Tricky. For the two Euro away games, manager Benny Webb, club physio Terry Vaudeville and Dog's agent Neil Veal had come up with a solution. They had got him to the venues by pedal bike. It took a long time, but at least he got there.

Then, after the Moscow match, with all Dog's domestic probs sorted, the time at last came for him to ride all the way to England. When Luke and the rest of the squad flew home, Dog and Terry V were setting out on their tandem. Just under three weeks later the two of them arrived at Ash Acre, Albion's ramshackle ground. That was five days ago...

"So this is good news, surely?" asked Uschi,

when Rodney had explained that far. "The Dog is in England. He will play tomorrow night, yes?"

Again Rodney, Luke and Frederick swapped glances. "Well – maybe," Luke told her. "You see, Dog hasn't really been in top condition since he arrived."

"Not a well man," said Frederick, shaking his head.

"It's like he's travel-sick or something," Rodney added. "Dizzy all the time. Headaches. His skin's a sort of greenish colour. No one knows what's up."

Uschi put her head on one side as this sank in. "So he might not be able to play against PSG, after all?" she asked. The other three shrugged. There was a pause. She tilted her head a bit more. Then she said, "There is something I do not understand, though. You say that Dog and Terry cycled from Moscow to England. Yet what happened when they came to the coast of France? Dog cannot travel by ship. So how did they cross the English Channel?"

For a third time, the man and two boys looked at one another. "Now *that*," said Rodney, "is the sixty-four thousand dollar question."

"But has no one asked Terry? Surely he must know?"

"He must do," Luke answered. "But he won't say a word about it."

"Well, that's not exactly true," Rodney corrected him. "Whenever anyone asks Terry about it, all he'll say is, 'Don't tell Dog that England isn't joined on to Europe!' Over and over again. And so far, no one has."

"Obviously something weird happened when they got to the Channel," Luke said, shrugging. "I guess we'll find out in the end what it was."

"Mystery," nodded Cool F.

"Come on, then," said Rodney, standing up and looking at his watch. "I'm feeling fine now. And Luke's mum will soon be putting the tea on the table. We don't want to be late for that, do we?" He shivered at the thought.

Frederick stood too. Luke followed, then leaned across towards Uschi. He was going to reach down for one of her cases. But the Girl from Germany, still sitting on them, got completely the wrong end of the stick. She jerked back her head, glared at him, then softly said, "Not here, Luke," and smiled that little smile.

She'd thought he was trying to kiss her!

Oh wow, thought Luke, stepping back sharply, I'm in even bigger trouble here than I'd thought.

4

The next morning – Thursday – Luke's mum drove Luke and Uschi to his school. As far as she was concerned, their German visitor would sit in on Luke's classes all that day, meet his friends and get a feel for English education.

No way! Thursday also happened to be UEFA Cup match-day. Benny Webb needed to put the full Albion squad through a final training session. And that meant Luke had to be at Ash Acre by ten o'clock. His headmistress knew all about that, of course. She came and got Luke out of his class herself when the taxi driver arrived to take him across town. (Frederick went straight to the ground from home. He lived with his older sister, and came and went just as he liked.)

Uschi put up her hand. "May I please accompany Luke?" she asked.

No, no, no, NO! Luke pleaded with his eyes at the head. It did no good.

"Yes, I don't see why not, Uschi," she said.

Then she smiled as the two kids followed her out of the classroom. "It'll be an education for you to see an old-fashioned English football ground from the inside. They don't make them like Ash Acre any more!"

"They wouldn't be allowed to," agreed the taxi driver, falling into step. "It's all going to be a very different kettle of fish up at the Majestic Stadium. Bet you can't wait to start displaying your unique skills on *that* lush turf – eh, Luke?"

"Sorry?" asked Luke. He hadn't heard the question because he'd been too busy trying to avoid all contact with Uschi in the narrow corridor.

"The spanking new ground that Mr Prince has built for Albion, Luke," the head answered, opening the door out on to the car park. "Are you looking forward to the grand opening? It's only a matter of days away now, isn't it?"

"Yes," said Luke. "Something like that." Albion were *meant* to be playing at the new 25,000 all-seater stadium before the end of the season. Jimbo had dearly wanted them to play PSG there that very night. But there had been all sorts of last-minute hitches – especially with the huge, retractable roof. To say that this made the player-chairman hopping mad was an understatement. He had been living on one leg for most of the past month.

"Off you go then, you two," said the head,

holding the taxi's rear door open. But Luke didn't fancy a twenty-minute trip in the back with Uschi. Already she'd started giving him those weird looks again. Smartly he opened the other door and nipped into the front seat instead.

"And Luke," said the head as she waved them off, "make sure Benny Webb gives you all plenty of shooting practice this morning. We can't have yet another nil-nil draw tonight. Remember: goals pay the rent."

The taxi driver rabbited on all the way to Ash Acre. Mainly about how he'd once given a ride to Martin Keown's hairdresser. It was pretty boring. But at least it saved Luke from having to twist around and chat to Uschi. He had the feeling, though, that her eyes were constantly boring into the back of his head. And when he started slipping into his disguise, she piped up at last:

"Why do you need your hunchback and dark glasses now, Luke? Surely you do not have to be unrecognizable to your fellow players?"

The driver laughed. "From the number of decent passes he gets from those others," he said, "I reckon half of 'em *don't* recognize him out on the park!"

"No," Luke explained, tugging down his baseball cap, "it's not the squad I need to hide from. Just the reporters and agents and everyone outside the ground. Once they get hold of you, they don't let you go without a fight."

"A fight?" Uschi almost growled. "If I were to be there, I would let no one ever harm *you*, Lukey."

"Well, as it happens," the driver pointed out, "I think you're in the clear today. Look, Mr Prince is giving a press conference over there in the car park."

As the taxi drew up and Luke and Uschi got out, no one was waiting at the main entrance to Ash Acre. Meanwhile a high-pitched rant could be heard above the row of players' cars. That was where the press and TV pack was gathered, feverishly jotting down every squeak that Jimbo – in full kit – made.

Luke couldn't catch many words but he sounded well mad. Not so much hopping now as practically in mid-air all the time. It seemed that the Majestic Stadium opening had been put back by *another* week. Jimbo had already sued the builders several times over for missing deadlines. In the end they would be paying *him* to get Albion's new home finished.

"Oooh," gasped Uschi as they stepped inside the hallowed portals of old Ash Acre. She was used to the magnificent Olympiastadion where Bayern played. There weren't great sheets of rusting, graffiti-sprayed metal all over the front of *that*. There was no peeling paint, or a stink of ancient onions and threadbare carpet in the foyer either. And she hadn't yet been shown the weed-infested, standing-only terraces on three sides of the pitch. One of the secretaries waved from behind a cracked glass panel, got up from her desk and started to come out.

"I can see why the club must move from *here*," Uschi went on.

"Oh, it's not a bad old place really," Luke told her, heading off down the corridor towards the dressing-rooms. It always bugged him when strangers knocked Ash Acre. OK, so it wasn't state-of-the-art. But one way or another, Luke had had some of the best times of his life here. "See you, then."

"But it is so *small*!" Uschi panted – very close behind him.

He glanced back to see her almost wedged into the narrow corridor. "Hey," he said. "You can't come down here. This is the way to the dressing-rooms!"

Uschi's eyes flashed briefly then went dark with sorrow.

"You come with me, love," said the secretary from the corridor's other end. "I'll get you sorted. What about a nice hot drink and a snack?"

Briefly Luke paused before pressing on down to the dressing-room. Should he warn Uschi about the club's petrol-flavoured tea and ghastly burgers? No, she wasn't stupid. No one in their right mind would touch that stuff. On he went.

5

"Headless!" cried Terry Vaudeville as soon as Luke stepped inside the door marked Home Team.

"*Headless!*" sang out everyone else in a chorus, pointing Luke's way.

Luke rolled his eyes and crossed to his peg. Headless Hero was another one of his nicknames. (Headless, because in most of his adverts he appeared only from the neck down.) Terry went on squeezing, rubbing and karate-chopping the bottom of the player lying face-down on the physio's bench: the young winger Darius Aldershot, a recent graduate of the club's Centre of Excellence.

"What's up, Dazza?" asked Luke. He seemed to be in complete agony. Too much, anyway, to be able to answer.

"I'm tryin' to get the circulation going again," Terry explained. "He just took a bit of a whack." He nodded to where full-back Craig Edwards sat sheepishly nursing a battered-looking pineapple.

"It's all down to me," Craig admitted. "You know how Carl always likes a pre-match hit from a pineapple, just to make sure he scores? Well, he hasn't got a goal for so long, I thought I'd bring along my own bit of fruit to give him an extra whack before training today. A surprise one, you know?"

"It certainly surprised Dazza," grunted veteran midfielder Michael "Half-Fat" Milkes.

"Yeah, well," shrugged Craig. "When they're bending down with jeans on, Carl and Daz look pretty similar. It's a mistake anyone could have made."

"But it was *you* that made it," boomed a big old bearded guy in a big old sheepskin coat – manager Benny Webb. Plainly fed up to the back teeth, he reached down and smacked Craig on the side of the head.

"Steady on, Benny!" Terry called out. "We don't wanna lose another one."

"You don't need to remind me of that," Benny called back. "I'm glad to see you've got here, Luke son. But look at the rest of us. Big Match Day and we've got hardly half a dozen in here. Chrissie's still not back from some fashion show he went to last night. Madman Mort's off doing a pilot for a Channel 5 late-night chat-show. I ask you – a goalkeeper: *chatting*! Dennis Meldrum's in London with Vealy, selling the film rights to this *novel* he's written with Craig..."

"Er, still writing, actually," Craig corrected him, rubbing his head. "That's why I didn't go with them today. I was up half the night on Chapter Twenty-Three."

Benny shook his great shaggy head in disbelief.

"Then we've got the Dog too groggy to come in," sighed club captain Stuart "Gaffer" Mann. "Still conked out with his mystery illness. Shouldn't he see a doctor?"

Terry suddenly looked shifty, cleared his throat, and gave Darius an extra-hard bit of pummelling. "No. No need for doctors," he said. "Besides, the lad's gonna be all right for tonight. He told me that this morning when I rang him."

"He *told* you?" asked Trinidadian midfielder Narris Phiz. "How did he manage that, then?" It was a fair question. Dogan Mezir knew only seven words of English: "I am exceedingly pleased to meet you".

Terry winked and tapped his nose. Just then there was a knock at the door. Luke froze. Surely Uschi couldn't have done a runner from the refreshment area and tracked him down to here? Benny stomped over and opened the door.

"*No!*" Luke heard him roar – and so must everyone else inside Ash Acre. "No, no and no again! You're not filming inside this room and that's final! I don't care what it says in the contract you negotiated with Mr Prince at the start of the season! No one said a word about it to me. This dressing room is sacred territory. If I ever catch *any* of you in here, I'll … I'll…"

"Leave it, Benny," said Ruel Bibbo, going over and quietly closing the door. "They're not worth getting wound up about," said the big black ex-England striker who now ran the club's Centre of Excellence. "Not again, anyway."

"Flaming fly-on-the-wall documentary scum!" fumed Benny, stabbing a finger. "Bunch of Peepin' Toms, that's all they are! Why did Princey ever let 'em in?"

"Talking of our honoured player-chairman," said Carl Davey, slipping his shin-pads in, "is there *no* way we can keep him off the pitch tonight?"

Benny's face darkened. For a moment Luke thought he might be about to cry. "You all know my feelings on this matter," he said solemnly. "If it hadn't been for Mr Prince, our club would have gone bust last season. He saved our skin. So it's the least we can do to let him play," he paused, "when he's fit…"

"What?" cried Carl, suddenly hopeful. "You mean it's OK for us to nobble him in training this morning?"

"No chance there, I'm afraid, Carl," said Ruel. "He's straight off to town after his press conference. See a man about a lawsuit."

"This is *not* football as I know and love it," Benny wailed. "Fashion-shoots, chat-shows, films of novels, sick Armenian strikers, retractable roofs and lawsuits! How did it ever get to be like this? Whatever happened to—"

Again there was a knock at the door. Benny's beard seemed to stand on end. He rushed across the room faster than he ever had in his less-than-glorious playing days, tore back the door and let fly (on-the-wall): "*Look! I've told you lot to keep out of my face, right! I've just about*... Oh. Sorry, love. I thought you was... Oh, look. Don't cry, there's a good girl..."

Girl! Luke quivered. It *was* Uschi this time! He had to get out there before she steamrollered her way in and saw Darius Aldershot in his Y-fronts!

But when he stole up behind the Boss and peeked out, it wasn't Uschi sobbing in the corridor. It was a smaller, darker girl wearing a school uniform.

"I'm sorry, I'm s-s-sorry," she hiccuped. "I didn't know where to go. My n-n-name's Sara Briar and I'm here to d-d-do two weeks work experience..."

"Work experience?" said Benny. "Here? But you're a—"

"Girl," she sniffed. "I know. I applied to do a fortnight at the C-C-Castle Museum. But they got the papers mixed up. S-s-so I've been sent here. I th-th-think I'd better just go back to school."

"No, no," said Benny, putting a big sheepskin arm around her shoulders and offering her his own freshly-laundered handkerchief. "It doesn't matter how you've got here. You're at Castle Albion FC now and we'll do everything we can to fit you in somewhere. Football clubs exist for the whole community. We're not just big businesses. We don't just take from the people – we like to give back as well. So, Sara, we are proud to welcome you."

All the players behind him broke into a spontaneous round of applause.

"All right, you lot," Benny roared back over his shoulder. "That's enough of that! Get up on the pitch and do twenty laps! I'll be with you as soon as I've found this young lady something to do."

And off they all charged up the tunnel, with Luke leading the way.

6

Luke's mum *did* go to the Ideal Gnome Exhibition that evening – but not without a fight.

With less than an hour to go before kick-off, she was still stretched out on the sitting-room sofa. A headache had struck in mid-afternoon. However many aspirins Rodney fed her, she just couldn't *think* of travelling all the way to Birmingham. In the end, the poor guy had to lie through his teeth to shift her. Des Lynam, he said, had promised to put in an appearance. He was one hundred per cent certain to be there. In the flesh. It was also just possible that, with a bit of luck, she might even be able to go up and … shake his hand!

As soon as they chugged off in the Escort, Luke dashed upstairs. He kept a spare set of kit under his bed for emergencies like this. In a flash, he changed into it – wanting to be able to give his full attention to Benny's team-talk when he got to Ash Acre. Quickly he phoned the ground to say he was on his way. Then he put on his shades, baseball cap, hunchback and puffer jacket.

As he did so, he didn't have to keep an eye out for Uschi. Hours before, she had been picked up by the head for "a private little dinner". Luke knew what kind of dinner that would be. The finest fare Ash Acre could dish up. Gallons of petrol-flavoured tea and as many ghastly-burgers as she could eat. She had *loved* the stuff that morning. She'd even stunk out the taxi by bringing two extra burgers back to school afterwards, for lunch. But at least she was happy.

Luke was happy too as he stormed up Cranham Hill on his mountain bike. So much had been going on, he'd hardly had time to think about the match. But now this was it! UEFA Cup semi-final time! Games didn't come much bigger.

You couldn't tell from looking at the streets, though. Hardly anyone was about. But Luke knew why. Little Ash Acre's capacity was now a mere 12,000. Everyone who had a ticket – whether blue-and-white-hooped home fans or PSG's famous blue-and-red clad *hoolicools* – was already inside the ground. Everyone else was crowding around a TV set somewhere, ready to watch events unfold live on ITV, presented direct from Ash Acre by ... Des Lynam.

Just think – thought Luke – Des was *this close*

to Luke's mum. Yet now she was hurtling *away* from him at forty-five miles per hour. He winced. Old Rodney was really going to have to pay for that little white lie of his.

But that was still in the future. As Luke rode under the glare of the ageing floodlights on their great pylons, he made himself focus only on the football. Paris Saint-Germain! PSG from footie-mad France – currently riding high in their country's top division. PSG – where a flying young winger called David Ginola had first hit the world's headlines. PSG – once the home of all-time greats like superstriker George Weah and midfield maestro Juri Djorkaeff. PSG – 1996 *winners* of the old European Cup-Winners Cup, the competition that Albion would now be in if it hadn't merged with the UEFA Cup.

The fab French outfit didn't have any mega-stars in their line-up now. But they weren't going to be pushovers – as Benny had been warning all week. No French side was easy meat. France held the World Cup, for heaven's sake! While we were cranking out battling David Battys and itching-for-a-fight Paul Inces, *they* specialized in super-sleek Zinedine Zidanes and Emmanuel Petits. But sometimes you needed a bit of good old British grit in games like these. Maybe tonight Albion could mix some British spit with the French polish.

Luke locked up his bike and zipped into the ground – waving at the stewards and sold-out programme sellers who spotted him and wished him luck. The first person he saw in the foyer was Sara Briar, the work-experience girl. Helping out with lottery tickets for the half-time draw, she looked a whole lot happier than she had done that morning.

"Hi there," panted Luke with a smile. "Benny got you sorted then?"

"Yes thanks," she smiled back. "It's brilliant! All the best tonight, Luke!"

He grinned and trotted off to the dressing-room.

"...and finally, just remember this," Benny was saying as Luke slipped inside (*without* knocking on the door first). "I've told you all about this French lot – how good they are, how tricky they'll be to beat over two legs, all that stuff. But although they might be a bigger *club* than us, although they might have won more *trophies* than us, they are not – I repeat *not* – older than us!"

Everyone in the room frowned. Then the more senior players cast puzzled looks at Luke, at Frederick, at Keats Aberdeen, at Casper Franks – even at Chrissie and keeper Madman Mort – all of whom were still way short of twenty.

"Come again, Boss?" asked Gaffer Mann. "We've got to be the younger side."

"No, no, no!" spluttered Benny. "I don't mean right now! I mean in terms of *history*. Albion, as you all well know, was started up in...?" He paused to hear everyone shout out the answer. In the event, only one player knew it.

"Eighteen seventy-two," murmured Cool F, making a victory sign. "Respect to the club's Victorian founders."

"Spot on!" cried Benny, eyes alight. "And when do you think this bunch got started? I'll tell you when. *Nineteen seventy!* We're nearly a hundred years older than them. So tonight we've got *tradition* behind us! *We* are the true old hands here, however many Cup-Winners Cups this lot have won! It's *us* who's the more experienced team! Remember *that* as you enter this historic match!"

"Yeah, right," Luke heard Narris mutter to Half-Fat as everyone then stood up. "We've had a hundred years more experience of losing to the likes of Torquay United. That'll be a big help."

"Enjoy that team-talk?" Terry whispered up at the towering, still green-looking Dog, who was standing right next to Luke now. "Get a lot out of it, did you?"

"I am," the Dog murmured back, "exceedingly pleased to meet you."

"OK, I've said enough!" roared Benny. "This is do-or-die time lads. Go out there now and remind those Frenchies why we won the battle of Agincourt!"

"*Yeah-h-h-h-h-h!!!*" shouted everyone as they piled out into the corridor, all fired up for the fight.

"Agincourt, though?" said Carl, as they entered the tunnel. "That was an away leg, wasn't it?"

7

The cheer that greeted both teams was loud enough to make old King Henry V – the original winning skipper at Agincourt – twitch in his grave.

Luke had played in some pretty big games at Ash Acre. Against Villa, Newcastle and Liverpool in the FA Cup. Versus Turkey's Fenerbahce, Bayern Munich and Spartak Moscow in the UEFA Cup. But he'd never felt such an electrifying atmosphere. Unfortunately, the electricity hadn't made it all the way to the public address system.

"Tonight," began the announcer over the still-booming 12,000, "we would like to welcome the players, fans and officials of Paris Saint-Ger... phut ... fizz ... crackle ... *hummmmmmmmm*." And, in a deafening but thankfully brief storm of screeching feedback, that was as far as he got.

Without a PSG name-check over the tannoy, Luke glanced down the pitch to look at them kicking in. There, in front of their own standing *hoolicools*, Boulogne Boys and *Supras*, they stroked balls about in their greyish change strip. Funnily enough, like Albion's earlier UEFA opponents Bayern Munich, they too had Opel as shirt-front sponsors.

Luke thought he recognized a few of the faces. That was definitely Bernard Lama, ex-West Ham, in goal. And the big striker was Mickael Madar, who used to turn out for Everton. Then there were a couple of World Cup stars. That was the Brazilian Augusto Cesar, and that sleek guy bouncing the ball on his shoulders was Nigeria's Jay-Jay Okocha. And the bloke with the captain's armband was Ali Benarbia – according to Ben Webbia, he made the whole side tick... Oh wow, they did look a bit awesome. Still...

The ref blew his whistle, and up trotted Gaffer for the toss. As he did so, the noise from Albion's hardcore fans under the clock on the South Side terrace hit an all-time high. No one could sing louder than Supporters Club chairman Rocky Mitford. But that night, even his voice was just one among the many:

"Stand UP For The Albion!"
they sang.

"Stand UP For The Albion!!"
And then they all went up on tiptoe – because they were on their feet already, since there weren't any seats on the South Side. Luke looked over and waved. So did most of the rest

of the team. Only Jimbo Prince seemed not to be noticing anything around him. (No change there, then.)

He was standing on the halfway line, staring blindly at the PSG fans. It wasn't that his glasses had steamed up. They were crystal clear, and tied around the back of his corkscrew-haired head with a bit of blue-and-white string. This was his way of getting "on to the correct spiritual plane for the game ahead". Well, that was what his own personal faith-healer called it. As far as his team-mates were concerned, he just put himself into a kind of hypnotic trance. With a bit of luck, he would stay that way for the full ninety minutes. At least he wouldn't keep on getting in everyone else's way then, and giving away diabolical free kicks.

In theory, at least, Jimbo was playing up front alongside Carl – with Dog tucked in behind them in a withdrawn position. And behind *him*, from left to right, Chrissie, Half-Fat and Luke were strung out across midfield; while bringing up the rear were Craig, Gaffer and Dennis, with Frederick sweeping up behind them all, and Madman Mort in goal. Some managers played 4-4-2, some played 4-3-3. With Benny Webb it was 1-3-3-1-2. ("Is that what they call a Christmas Tree formation?" a reporter had asked him that morning. "No," Big Ben replied. "It's more what I'd call Iced Lolly With Two Bites Taken Out Near The Top.")

Gaffer won the toss, so Albion got to kick towards the away end for the first forty-five. That was just how they liked it. Then in the second half their own fans at the West End could suck the ball goalwards whenever Albion attacked.

But for the first quarter, neither side could really get a rhythm going. Maybe it was semi-final nerves, but no one seemed able to put his foot on the ball and play a measured pass. To be fair, Cool F managed it a couple of times. But on both occasions the player he picked out was Jimbo. Standing in acres of space just inside his own half, he clearly hadn't yet reached the correct spiritual plane to take an active part in the game. So the ball just cannoned off his shins.

Oddly for a team of their pedigree, PSG seemed in a trance themselves. Lama completely miskicked a back-pass. Two of their defenders collided in going for the same through-ball. Madar took a flick-on from Okocha, turned away from Gaffer, then lost his sense of direction and ran the ball straight into touch.

Their coach Philippe Bergeroo was giving them a right earful from the dug-out. It was all Greek to Luke, but the Spanish ref obviously knew French swear-words when he heard them. He kept looking over and wagging his finger. If Bergeroo kept it up though, he couldn't be banished to the tiny main stand behind. Every seat in it was taken, and nobody was likely to give one up. The ref would have to make him go and stand on the uncovered Town End terrace.

Twenty-five minutes passed. Thirty. And the mistakes just kept on coming. Luke and Frederick strung a couple of passes together. But whenever they tried to involve another Albion player, the move fizzled out fast. Jimbo *still* hadn't really moved from his spot near half-way, and for all the good he'd done, Dog might just as well have stayed rooted too. It was painful to see him wince and flinch every time he took a step. The man belonged in a bed. Benny could only be keeping him on because two PSG defenders followed him wherever he lurched. This gave more space to Carl. But that was precisely where the Pineapple Guy sent all three of his first-half goal-attempts – into space, quite astronomically high and wide of Lama's goal.

None of this was what Des Lynam, Clive Tyldesley, Big Ron Atkinson, Barry Venison and everyone else from ITV had come to Ash Acre for. Viewers must have been switching off in droves – however hard the men with the mikes tried to look on the bright side. There are only so many times that people can listen to, "Well, Ron, at least PSG haven't grabbed an all-important away goal." And in all honesty, that was the only thing that *hadn't* gone wrong for Albion – yet.

As half-time drew closer, the fans were probably making less noise – all together – than Benny Webb down on the touchline. Waving his arms, stamping his feet, throwing back his head, he could have been giving another history lesson for all the sense he was making. But he didn't look a happy manager. Luke could just imagine what an ear-bashing he was going to give them all at the break. Tea-cups flying at the wall. The lot.

And maybe this awful idea finally got him going. Okpara had sliced the ball into touch midway into the PSG half. Dog staggered over to take the throw-in. That wasn't his job, but no one on the Albion side tried to stop him. At least the ball would then go to someone who might be able to kick it straight. The player in question – haring forward as if he'd been fired from a catapult – was Luke.

Benarbia slid in to try to dispossess him, but Luke made a monkey of him with a sudden change of direction. The rest of the PSG defence looked a bit flat-footed as well – and all their eyes were now on Luke as he homed in on their penalty area. So none of them noticed Frederick arrowing in from the back.

Luke saw him, though. He lobbed a lovely little ball deep into the box, right over Augusto

Cesar – who spun around in despair, thrust out a leg and sent Cool Frederick flying in a dive that Jurgen Klinsmann would have been mightily proud of. Only this time the defender really did make contact. In the fracas that followed, Frederick had the blood and studmarks down his right thigh to prove it.

When all the argy-bargy was over, and Terry had sponged down Frederick's leg, there really were only two decisions that the ref could take. One, Cesar had to be red-carded. Two, Albion had to have a penalty. And these were exactly the two decisions that he took. Off stomped Cesar. Then up stepped Albion's penalty king to place the ball on the spot. Who was this player?

A Sensation without a Stud. A Hero minus a Head. Lukey, Lukey, Lukey Green!

8

The Boulogne Boys behind Lama's goal could hiss and honk till the cows came home. They could scream "Southgate!" (Or "Zouthgit!") at him till their throats went hoarse. Luke calmly took three steps forward, put trainer to leather – and there was the ball threatening to break through the net. And the more often they showed action replays on ITV, the harder it was to tell if the ex-international keeper was diving to try and save it or just to get out of its way.

Albion one, PSG nil! The dreadful deadlock had been broken! A goal, a goal!

"No Boots! No Head!!

He Leaves Them All For Dead –

Lukey GREEN, Lukey GREEN!"

bellowed the Southsiders.

Luke's grateful team-mates picked him up and carried him all the way back to the Albion half. Not one of them had doubted he would hammer it home. But there was still a surprise.

One so big, it almost shut up the wild Albion faithful.

"The scorer of tonight's first goal," declared the stadium announcer as clear as a bell, "was Albion's sensational Number Seven – Luke Green!"

The players looked at one another, dumb-founded. The announcement had been absolutely, crystal-palace clear! No *phhts*, no *hmmms*, no *bzzz*'s. It was like being in a proper football ground!

"NO Dodgy Tannoy!" roared Rocky and Co.

"We Have Got NO Dodgy Tannoy!"

Then, fired up by the goal, Albion almost snatched a second before the break.

Frederick dispossessed Madar just outside the centre-circle, and sprayed a perfect ball out wide to Chrissie. The super-slaphead took two strides forward and slung over a cross aimed for Carl. *Aimed* for Carl. But it wasn't one of Chrissie's more accurate efforts. Instead of swinging in for the on-lumbering Carl, it swung away towards Lama's goal. A goal which Lama had dashed out of, expecting to intercept a cross. The keeper twisted around to look back in agony as the ball sailed towards his net. But, at the last moment, it curved away even further, hit a post, and rebounded into his grateful arms.

The fans of both sides were still getting their breath when the ref blew for half-time. At once the announcer began to reel off a list of other half-time scores, without the slightest blip or hiss from the tannoy. Amazing!

Benny met the players with a silent, stony face as they all trooped into the dressing-room. All the players except Jimbo, that was.

"Where the flippin' heck's the chairman?" Benny stormed at last.

"Having a word with his faith-healer in the tunnel, Boss," said Ruel. "I think she's making a few adjustments to his spiritual plane."

"Does that mean he'll actually *move* in the second half?" asked Narris.

"Never mind about him!" Benny ranted. "Most of you lot were like the Living Dead out there! I've never seen such a shambles! OK, so we're a goal up now, thanks to Luke and Frederick. But as for the rest of you – *I* could've put in a better forty-five!" He turned to Dog. "And *you*, Dog, son – you look finished."

The big Armenian goal-machine sadly shook his shaggy, long-haired head. "I am exceedingly," he murmured, "pleased to meet you."

"Don't worry, son," Benny told him. "You did your best. But I'm putting Casper on instead of you for the second half. All right, Casper? Strip off."

For the next five minutes, as everyone sipped

their half-time tea, Benny gave all the players in turn a rocket. (All except Luke and Frederick, of course.) When he'd got it out of his system, Gaffer spoke up.

"Fair play, Boss," he said. "We deserved that. We're playing like drains. But it doesn't help to have only ten men. For all he's done, Jimbo might as well not be out there." The others all nodded and muttered their agreement.

Benny shook his head. "You've got to work *around* him," he said. "And look at it this way: it could be worse. He could be buzzin' about like a headless chicken near our penalty box, giving away dangerous free kicks by the job lot. And anyway, *they*'ve only got ten men now too."

The others shrugged. The boss had a point. They had to be grateful for small mercies. Then it suddenly went quiet. Everyone sat twiddling their thumbs. "Tell you what, though," piped up Keats. "Somebody's fixed that tannoy."

"Yeah," smiled Terry V, "and you'll never guess who it was."

"Jimbo's faith-healer?" suggested Half-Fat.

"No chance," Terry grinned. "It was that little lassie we've got on work experience. She took one look at the wiring and sorted it in a flash. Smart girl."

"*Well* smart," Chrissie Pick agreed, surprisingly loudly. The others glanced his way, but he was nodding at the wall with a faraway look on his face. "I saw her when I got to the ground this evening. She smiled at me. Such a *big* smile..."

"That's enough of that!" bellowed Benny, tossing a ball at Chrissie's glistening head to bring him back down to Earth, or at least to Planet Football. "Save your canoodling till after the match. And the rest of you – forget about novels and chat-shows and catwalks and supermarket openings. Just get out there and do what you're meant to do best: putting the fear of God up French footballers!"

"*Right, Boss!*" his eager squad bellowed back. Then out they charged, mad keen to do in the second half everything that they hadn't done in the first.

And by the second half's midway point, they had done one *very* new thing. They had given away a goal. Not just once, but twice.

9

To say that *Albion* gave away two goals isn't strictly accurate. Sure, football is a team game. All for one and one for all. The team that plays together, stays together. But sometimes, for better or for worse, key moments in a game are all down to a single player. A Michael Owen. A Ronaldo. A Jimbo Prince.

For it was the player-chairman, and the player-chairman alone, who handed PSG two priceless away goals. Luke had noticed as the second half started that Jimbo had a weird look on his face. Sort of ... mad. It was anyone's guess what his personal faith-healer had said or done to him in the interval. But clearly she'd said or done *something*.

He rushed about the pitch like a boy possessed. Not necessarily in pursuit of the ball. In fact, more often than not he seemed to be running *away* from where the action was. Which was a very good thing, compared to what came later. He was chattering to himself all the time too. Now and then as he buzzed past, Luke caught a few words. They sounded like: *I am a football genius... I can do anything on this pitch... There is nothing I cannot do...*

And in a way, he was right. He proved it in the fifty-seventh minute. That was when he did what no one else in either team (or even in the crowd) could possibly have done. He scored an own goal from twenty-five yards out – with an overhead kick.

For the rest of that week, when his mum wasn't around, Luke kept sneaking looks at the action replay on the video of the game that Rodney had secretly made. It took about ten viewings before he fully understood how it had happened. At the time, it was nothing but a crazy, incomprehensible blur.

It started with Albion on the attack, as they had been ever since the restart. Narris fed a ground-pass through to Luke, who chipped a high ball to the far post where Casper had made a great run. Franksy met it full on the forehead and nodded it tantalizingly across the six-yard box. Carl threw himself forward to direct a low, hard header at goal. Lama dived, and somehow he managed not only to stop the shot, but also to gather it into his body with one hand.

But instead of milking the crowd's applause like most keepers do, Lama leapt to his feet and hoofed the ball high upfield. No one was expecting that. Not even his own team-mates. None of them was even *near* the Albion half. There were just three players in that part of the field. Madman, on the edge of his box – still cursing Lama's save from Casper's header. Gaffer, who was standing, hands on hips, just inside the centre-circle. And – for no particularly good reason – Jimbo, who was buzzing about between them.

Gaffer tilted back his head and watched the ball sail over him. He had no worries at all. Two bounces and it would be in Madman's arms. Meanwhile Madman stopped effing and blinding and patiently waited for it to come to him.

Which it never did. Jimbo saw to that. After the first bounce he jumped to try and trap it on his chest – way too soon. In doing so, he skidded and toppled backwards. And, as the ball dropped down, he lashed out with his right foot before falling flat on his back. He had never made a more perfect contact. The ball rocketed over his shoulder, fizzed past Madman and smashed into the net off a post. Albion one PSG one! The visitors had their priceless away goal!

Three sides of Ash Acre fell silent. No one said a word to Jimbo. Jimbo said nothing to anyone. Everyone on the Albion bench put their heads in their hands. It would have been better if they had left them there. That way, they wouldn't have seen Jimbo give away the free kick that led to the second PSG strike.

It came after another period of heavy Albion pressure. The other nine outfielders were all playing their socks off now. No question of letting that awful own goal get them down. Luke had a drive headed off the line. Casper sent two headers just wide. Chrissie went on a mazy run that ended with him scooping a shot just over Lama but also just over the crossbar. It seemed only a matter of time before they hit the net again. Then in came Jimbo.

Benny had been waving at him to get out of the Albion half. Even Jimbo couldn't beat Madman from beyond the halfway line. But he was in a world of his own. Still buzzing, still chattering, he was deep in his own half when Okocha received a long throw-out from Lama, turned past Half-Fat, and began to dribble towards Jimbo. And Jimbo just didn't see him coming. Literally.

Okocha pushed the ball to one side of him, then started to run around the other. Jimbo chose that moment to go buzz-about again – straight into the Nigerian. Okocha made a meal of the dive. (Jimbo really wasn't big enough or strong enough to send him flying.) But it *was* a foul – just outside the box – and the ref *did* have to give a free kick. For a blissful moment it looked as if he might red-card JP as well. But no such luck. All he got was a load of finger-wagging. Then it was just a matter of keeping him out of Madman's defensive wall.

Luke managed to escort the player-chairman out of the danger zone. But then he could only watch in despair as Okocha stepped up and curled a beauty into the top of Madman's net. Albion one PSG two! And as far as everyone connected with Albion was concerned, PSG stood for Pretty Stupid Geek: Jimbo!

After that, there was no way back for the home side. They huffed and they puffed but they couldn't blow PSG's defensive house down. With two goals under their belts, all the Frenchmen wanted to do was kill off the game. Which they did pretty successfully until the eighty-fourth minute, when all of a sudden – like Darren Anderton after surgery – it briefly roared back to life.

Unfortunately for Albion, the flurry of activity was at their own end of the pitch. And Jimbo wasn't even involved this time. He, like everyone else in blue hoops, was desperately pushing forward for an equalizer. But as every TV commentator on earth will tell you, that makes a team vulnerable to an attack on the break.

Benarbia in the PSG midfield knew that. A bit further forward, Madar did too. So when, after an Albion corner, the skipper nicked the ball away from Craig near the edge of his own box, he looked up and saw only three men between him and the distant Madman: Madar, Dennis and Gaffer. Quick as a flash he played the ball up to Madar, and set off on his quickest sprint of the night.

Madar understood. Instead of trapping the ball, he played the sweetest one-two with Benarbia. His pass slid right between Dennis and Gaffer. Neither could get to the ball before Benarbia rocketed through, took it in his stride and lashed a pearler past Madman into the far corner. Albion one, PSG three!

That was it. Game, set and match. The *hoolicools* went potty at the Town End. Droves of Albion fans streamed out of the ground. Benny's beard went even whiter. "And the scorer of PSG's third goal of the evening," boomed the announcer over the now-perfectly-working public address system, " was—"

"Oh Do Shut UP!"

Rocky and the Southsiders shouted back, almost raising the ancient rusty roof above their heads.

10

Luke didn't feel great the next day. Nor did Rodney. And it wasn't just a case of the blues from losing to PSG. He'd also had to deal with the fall-out from the trip to the *Ideal Gnome Exhibition*.

Luke's mum had *not* been amused by that. Apparently, all the gnomes on show had been of a very poor quality. (But what did a high quality gnome look like?) Then, of course, a certain Mr Lynam had failed to put in an appearance. And, on the drive back home, Rodney's Ford Escort had broken down on the motorway.

"Believe me," he whispered to Luke and Uschi as they left for school on Friday, "you really did *not* want to be there while we waited for the AA guy to turn up. It wasn't just headaches and moaning. She actually started whacking me. Here, on the arm. I'm all bruises under this shirt. And *then*, when the AA bloke came, he had his radio tuned in to your game! I was terrified she'd hear your name. But I guess she just blocked out all the sound."

Luke pulled a pained face in sympathy. Uschi did too. (Uschi did just about *everything* Luke did, short of following him into the boys' toilets at school.)

"Anyway, look," said Rodney in a louder voice. "You know your dad's getting back into the country today, don't you? He'll pick you both up straight from school. He's going to take you out for dinner, then bring you back here. OK?"

"OK," nodded Luke. "See you later." He lowered his voice. "And good luck with Mum."

The day dragged badly at school. Frederick didn't show at all – he was such an ace student, the head let him come and go as he pleased. Luke wished *he* hadn't turned up either. It wasn't just the other kids laughing about the PSG result. The teachers gave him all sorts of stick too. Mr Taft in Biology kept on for so long that in the end Uschi shot to her feet. "Sir," she blazed, "had you been at the game you would know that, over the ninety minutes, Albion were easily the better side! Two unfortunate errors proved extremely costly. That is all. And as for Luke, he played out of his skin for the total ninety minutes. Thank you!"

That was fair enough. But when she sat down, she touched Luke's hand lovingly with hers. Her face was all fuzzy with hero-worship. For a moment he thought she was going to take him on to her knee and console him further. Luckily the bell went just in time.

When they finally escaped from school, Luke's dad was waiting outside. It was hard to miss him. He was sitting behind the wheel of a basically yellow van, with hippie-style flowers and rainbows painted all over it. Luke's dad's antique baggy clothes were even more multi-coloured. "Hey there, Lukey baby!" he cried as his son climbed in. "And you must be Uschi! Right on, man!"

"Good afternoon, Mr Green," said Uschi. "It is pleasant to meet you."

"Oh wow, just call me TAFKAG," he smiled, jerking the van into motion and heading off towards his hotel just outside town.

TAFKAG stood for "The Artist Formerly Known As Green". Luke's dad was a singer-songwriter-guitarist who'd spent most of his career trying to get a proper recording contract. And frankly, until the previous year, he'd never got close. Even Luke could see why. He loved his dad to death, but he couldn't sing, couldn't write for toffee (unless you liked songs about "concrete geraniums" or "heavy-metal custard") and he seemed to break more strings on his guitar than he played. These were drawbacks for a singer-songwriter-guitarist.

But then he was roped in to write and record

a Cup Final single for the Albion. "Castle Rap" – featuring a killer spoken-word section from Cool F – shot to Number One in the UK *and* in fourteen other countries. They were mostly quite small countries, admittedly, but TAFKAG was at last on his way. With Neil Veal as his manager, he signed a multi-album deal with a major label. And in the past year he'd done concert tours in Australia, Scandinavia, Guinea-Bissau and Uruguay – among other places. It didn't matter to him that most of his audiences thought he was a comedian. As long as he had the chance to "get some beautiful musical thoughts across to the people" he was happy.

"So sorry I missed the game last night," he said, pulling up sharp at some traffic lights, and making a stack of amps and speakers topple over in the back. "Didn't get in from Liechtenstein till midnight. But the guys at the hotel video'd it for me. We'll run the whole thing through before dinner."

"I'm not sure that's a good idea," mumbled Luke. He was already feeling van-sick, and didn't fancy watching Jimbo's Horrorshow all over again. But once they got to the hotel, that's exactly what the three of them did. It wasn't a pretty sight. In fact it looked far worse on the small screen. Even TAFKAG, the chirpiest bloke on earth, looked a bit depressed afterwards.

"OK then," he said, "I'll slip into a new kaftan and we'll go get some grub."

He'd booked a table in the hotel restaurant. It was quite a posh gaff, and pretty crowded for so early in the evening. Luke noticed a few heads turning as they came in. Not for him. He had his dark-glasses-and-baseball-cap disguise on. No, they were checking out TAFKAG. His dad usually had that effect, but he *was* fairly weird-looking.

Most of the menu seemed to be in French, so none of them really knew what they were ordering. But when the food came it was fine.

"So how's Benny gonna turn this around?" TAFKAG asked. "What's he gonna do about old Jimbo? How's he gonna get the Dog back on song? And – much more to the point – how's he gonna get *you* to Paris for the vital second leg?"

"Ah," Uschi sighed. "Paris. The city of romance." She gazed at Luke as if she was about to melt, and he could have sworn she brushed a foot along his shin under the table. Thank the Lord he had only two more days of her.

"Search me," he gulped, shrugging at his dad. "Rodney's trying to come up with a plan. But after his plan for *last* night, I'm not too hopeful."

"And there's nothing I can do, dude," TAFKAG said. "Not till you get to Paris, anyway. I'm just touching base with you here. Tomorrow

I'm off on a ten-date European tour. Tirana, Warsaw, Oslo, Bucharest – you name it. But as luck would have it I wind up, on the night before the game, doing a gig in Paris!"

"Ah," Uschi sighed again. "Paris. The city—"

"So you'll be able to see the second leg?" Luke asked quickly, pulling his shins back in case Uschi started brushing again. TAFKAG nodded so excitedly that his green and red polka-dotted headband came down over his eyes. As he pulled it back up, Luke saw that more people than ever were staring their way.

"You've clocked it too, have you?" grinned TAFKAG. "All these guys giving me the once-over? I get that a lot now. Price of fame, man. Look, here comes the manager. Guess he'll ask me to give them a couple of tunes. I'm up for it."

The black-suited manager stopped at their table, a smarmy smile on his face. "I'm terribly sorry to disturb your meal, sir," he said to Luke's dad, "but some of the other guests are finding your ... ahem ... *clothing* a little too ... ah ... *loud*. It seems to be putting them off their food. Would you mind returning to your room and finding something a little easier on the eye, and ... er ... stomach?"

"No sweat," replied TAFKAG, blushing and standing at once. "No sweat there at all!" The manager thanked him and smarmed off.

"I could be some time," TAFKAG said to Luke and Uschi. "All my gear's like this. I think I'll have to nip across to the Mall opposite and get myself a suit. *Ciao!*"

And before Luke could say a word, he was gone. And Luke was all alone with Uschi. He felt a foot slowly brush up and down his shin. "*Paris...*" she said.

11

On Saturday afternoon Albion were at home to York City. There was no chance that Luke could play. It was Uschi's last full day in England, and his mum had lined up a "special treat" for her. Or rather, it was a special treat for herself, but it involved dragging Uschi, Luke and Rodney along too.

The AA man had done a good job on the Ford Escort. So Rodney was able to drive the four of them all the way to Blenheim Palace, just outside Oxford. They didn't get to see inside the Palace itself. Normally Luke wouldn't have minded that at all. He liked History about as much as he liked the smell of Madman's socks after a game. But it drizzled with rain right through the afternoon. So by the time they had walked all round the massive grounds – admiring the lake, the trees, the sheep – he was soaked through.

Even then, they didn't take shelter. There was a garden centre to be investigated – at great length. Forget about *Ideal Gnomes*. This was where Luke's mum got her biggest buzz. The other three could almost hear her fizzing and humming with ecstasy as she lingered among the herbaceous plants and pots, the roses and the lavender, the stacked-up bags of fertilizer.

And as if that wasn't bad enough, Luke *also* had to keep stepping sharply sideways. This was because, whenever his mum or Rodney weren't looking, Uschi kept doing her level best to link her fingers through his. Did the girl never give up? He hadn't given her an ounce of encouragement since she'd arrived. But she seemed to be getting *more* fixated on him with every hour that passed.

At one point he did manage to get away. He spotted a butterfly house, and suggested taking a look. At least it was dry in there. But Uschi shivered with horror. "These creatures, *ach* – they terrify me! All flitter-flitter-flitter! And with those horrid little prongs on their heads. Oh Luke, *nein, nein*!"

"Right then," said Luke. "I'll check it out on my own. See you later."

Once safely inside, he saw another youngish visitor listening in to a radio on earphones. He had a replica Spurs shirt on under his anorak. "Excuse me, please," said Luke, tapping him on the arm. "You haven't heard any of today's football results, have you?"

"Just listening in now, mate," he replied, eyes closed as he concentrated. "Man U won, Arsenal won, Leeds drew, Liverpool lost, Coventry got hammered..."

"Yes, yes," said Luke. "But what about Division Three? Castle Albion against York?"

"One-one," came the immediate reply, his eyes still shut. "Frederick Dulac put the home side one up in the forty-third minute from a direct free kick. Then it was all York till the seventy-seventh minute when a Madman Mort clearance took a cruel deflection off Jimbo Prince to secure the visitors a well-earned equalizer."

"Cheers," said Luke glumly. One point wasn't really enough. Albion *had* to win their home games if the spectre of relegation wasn't going to rise up again.

On rejoining the others, he slipped a sweet-wrapper to Rodney with the score written on it. "Oh *no!*" gasped Rodney, causing Luke's mum to throw a very strange look over her shoulder. But she didn't snap or ask him what was up.

"Wow," whispered Luke, "she's in a *really* good mood."

"I know," Rod whispered back. "She's loving every minute of this trip. I think I should make the most of it, don't you? Start sounding her out about Paris?"

Luke swallowed hard. Then he stepped

briskly aside as he felt Uschi's probing fingers. "Can't you tell *me* your plan first?" Luke hissed to Rodney, afraid that it would be as bad as his *Ideal Gnome* scam. "Maybe we should discuss it."

"Trust me," Rodney winked, then he stepped up to Luke's mum's side. She was queuing at a counter, waiting to pay for all the plants and seeds she'd collected. Luke and Uschi crept up behind them to listen in.

"I was just wondering, dear," Rodney began, "if maybe we could do with a little break? A little *foreign* break? Somewhere with lovely gardens. Like ... Paris?"

"Paris..." Uschi echoed softly. Luke just stepped aside. He was too confused to say anything to her. What was Rodney *up* to here? He was supposed to be getting *Luke* to Paris, not his mum! Oh, he was making a right horlicks of this.

"We could go, I thought, for a couple of nights," Rod bashed on, even though Luke's mum hadn't said a word. "Quite soon...? Maybe on a ... Tuesday?"

No, no, no, Luke thought. He's blowing this completely. A Tuesday? But the game was on the Thursday! Yet still his mum didn't say a word back. And, when the queue moved forward, she stayed rooted. Had she turned to stone, or what? Then Luke saw that she was looking, spellbound, past the counter. He followed her line of vision, and saw why.

Her eyes were fixed on a life-sized cardboard cut-out of Des Lynam doing one of his gardening ads. Without blinking, she pointed to it and said to Rodney in a small, determined, but quivering voice, "*I ... want ... that!*"

Well, thought Luke, at least she hadn't heard Rod's nutty suggestion. When Des Lynam got involved – even a cardboard replica of him – *nothing* else mattered.

An ugly scene followed, as Luke's mum offered up to forty pounds for the cut-out. The cashier kept telling her it wasn't for sale, and finally had to call the manager. He threatened to bar Luke's mum from the centre if she didn't take no for an answer. She argued a bit, stamped her foot a bit, then moaned *a lot.*

Two hours later, as they turned off the motorway for home, she was still whining on about her lost cardboard Des. Rodney took them on a winding route through town, just so she wouldn't get even a glimpse of Ash Acre. But from the back seat, Luke and Uschi got a glimpse of something else.

There, outside *MacDonald's*: large as life and twice as bald – Chrissie Pick. And Chrissie being Chrissie, he had female company. As Rodney drove past, Luke and Uschi twisted around to see which supermodel it was this time.

But it was no Kate Moss! The girl he was taking in his arms was little Miss Fixit Sara Briar – getting in some work experience that she *hadn't* expected!

But nor did Luke expect what happened next. The sight of Chrissie and Sara smooching must have been just too much for Uschi. She flipped. Twisting back around, she went for broke and lunged at Luke, aiming her puckered lips at his.

And Luke screamed.

He wasn't proud of that afterwards. Boys of his age aren't mean to scream. But boys of his age don't usually have Uschis looming up at them. Rodney screeched the Escort to a halt. "What's wrong? What's wrong?" cried Luke's mum, struggling out of her seatbelt and turning as Uschi sat back.

"Cramp!" Luke lied, with his face screwed up in mock pain. "Here, in my leg!"

"Cramp in your leg?" said his mum suspiciously. "That's what footballers get, isn't it?"

"No, I mean my arm!" Luke corrected himself. "My shoulder! Aaaarrggghhhh!"

"My goodness," said his mum, turning back. "What a lot of fuss about nothing! Now, what was I talking about before I was so rudely interrupted?"

"Des Lynam, dear," Rodney reminded her, restarting the car.

12

At two o'clock on Sunday afternoon, Luke, Frederick and Rodney saw Uschi safely on to her plane back to Germany. Luke insisted on staying at the airport until they saw it take off. "I just want to be absolutely sure that it's all over," Luke explained, "that she's gone, disappeared, *for ever*."

"Hmm," said Rodney as the plane began to taxi down the runway. "Well, she's on her way now. But it didn't seem to me that she was going *for ever*."

"Me neither," nodded Cool F.

Luke said nothing, but he knew what they meant. Uschi hadn't laid another finger on him since his backseat scream. (Amazingly, she'd seemed to believe he really did have cramp.) But she'd been looking at him even more weirdly than before. A knowing, almost smug, sort of look. And when the time had come for him to say goodbye, she'd flashed him a broad smile and said, "No, Luke. Not goodbye. Just *au revoir.*" Luke was terrible at French, but even he knew that meant "until next time". Then, as she went off, she'd mouthed something else at him. One word. He didn't have a clue what it was.

Over the next few days he tried to put her out of his mind. But when he forgot about her in the day, she came back to haunt his dreams – eyes closed, lips puckered. If she'd just packed in trying to kiss him, Luke thought, they could have got on OK. As it was, she remained his very own PSG – Pretty Scary German.

On Wednesday evening, however, something happened to sweep Uschi right out of his thoughts. Albion won a league match! It was way up north in Hartlepool, and Luke's mum needed him to help her weed the lawn, so again he couldn't get away to play. He went to bed early, though, and listened to the local radio commentary under his duvet.

Two good things were clear at once. One: Jimbo wasn't in the side. (He'd had to fly to Indonesia for an emergency business meeting.) Two: the Dog was finally back on song. He tore the 'Pool defence to shreds, scored with two cracking volleys, and Albion ran out three-nil winners. Precious, precious points!

So when Luke arrived by taxi at Ash Acre for training on Thursday morning, he expected a party atmosphere in the dressing-room. How wrong he was.

Half the squad wasn't there – including Frederick. Most of the rest were still in their street clothes. And every one of them was sitting bolt upright on the bench, arms folded, jaws set. They were all looking dead ahead too, as if they were afraid to look towards the bath area. So Luke looked that way at once. And standing there he found Benny, Tel – and a small, smiling, middle-aged woman in a pale green buttoned-up coat with matching handbag.

A *woman*! In the Albion dressing-room! The most sacred of all-male places – a No Go Area even to fly-on-the-wall TV documentary teams!

"OK, Luke, sit yourself down," said Benny wearily. "Get changed after, son. As you can all see, we've got a ... guest in here with us this morning." Still no one really dared to look her way. "I'd like to introduce you to Mr Prince's own personal faith-healer. Lads, say hello to Mrs Doris Plunkett."

"Hello – er – Mrs Plunkett," said all the players in a low, embarrassed mumble.

"Before he flew off to Indonesia," Benny explained, "Mr P arranged for Mrs Plunkett to make this here visit. He thinks that, well, after the way you played against PSG, some of you might – um – benefit from a private chat with her. Raise your spirits, like. Air any problems you might have, footballin' or otherwise..."

"I've got a footballing problem, Boss," said

Narris, shooting up his hand but still staring dead ahead. "It's to do with one of our players who's not even here today but who keeps on fouling up *everything* for the rest of—"

"Yeah right, Narris," Terry V cut in quickly. "I think we'll knock that one on the head right there, eh?" Everyone nodded sadly. There was no point in badmouthing Jimbo to someone who would probably go straight back and tell him. And even that wouldn't do any good. Jimbo's belief in his own ability was total. Whatever anyone else said, he truly believed that he was a classy footballer. Which he was. Tenth class. Fiftieth class. A millionth class.

"Mr Prince also arranged for half the squad to be at his lab today," Benny continued through gritted teeth. "Apparently he's going to produce a live action computer game based on this club – *VirtuAlbion...*"

"Oh *cool*!" cried games-mad Keats Aberdeen before he could stop himself.

Benny glared at him. "This will involve you lot 'modelling' for it," he went on. "Whatever that means. The rest of you will have to go to the lab tomorrow."

Luke felt really sorry for the boss. Computers meant nothing to him. He didn't know his mouse from his e-mail. He didn't even understand why Jimbo had re-named the Manager's Notes page in the programme *Webbsite*. And

71

he clearly wasn't overjoyed at having a faith-healer interfering with his lads' training.

"OK then, look," Benny finished off. "Let's go out and do a bit on the pitch. Then Mrs Plunkett will be in my office, for any of you to go and chat to."

"I just want to do for you lads what I'm doing for Mr Prince," Mrs P beamed.

The players did look at her then – in utter amazement and alarm. "Do you – er – *know* about football, Mrs Plunkett," Craig dared to ask.

"Oh yes!" she replied, nodding like mad. "Both my sons play Subbuteo. And I like the Arsenal. Their shirts are such a lovely shade of red, aren't they?"

Blank-faced, all the players nodded back.

"You know," she told them, "I can feel such a positive, healthy vibe in here already. I'm *sure* I can put you all on the correct spiritual plane."

Luke glanced at Benny. He could see exactly what sort of a plane the boss wanted to put Mrs P on. The sort of plane that *he* had put Uschi on at Heathrow – with a one-way ticket and no passport. "All right then, Mrs P. I'll show you to my office. Then these lads can get themselves changed."

"Oh, don't mind me," she giggled. "I'm only interested in the *soul*, not the body!" And with that, she plonked herself down on the bench. She was staying.

13

Luke didn't hang about after training. Without showering, he pulled his school clothes on over his kit, just in case Mrs Plunkett decided to pop into the dressing-room again. Then he hared straight out to the waiting taxi.

He thought he heard a female voice calling after him as he left. But he didn't look back. It could have been Mrs P, and she *really* gave him the creeps. For the rest of that day in school, he shivered every time he thought of her big-eyed smile. Benny Webb was almost certainly doing the same thing.

The boss had seemed to get more and more wound-up during training. For him, there was just too much *stuff* going on around the club now. And when he took a series of penalties against Madman but hit the fly-on-the-wall cameramen four times, Luke couldn't help thinking it wasn't entirely accidental.

At going-home time Luke linked up with Cool F. They'd already arranged to go to Frederick's place to work on some drama homework together. "How did it go up at Jimbo's lab this morning?" Luke asked him.

"Rude," the Cool One replied, which Luke was fairly sure meant good. "They're gonna do you after the French trip."

"Oh, right. Well, training wasn't great..." he began. But then his attention was distracted by a guy in a tracksuit, waving from a parked blue Metro.

"Hello, Terry," said Luke in surprise, approaching the open driver's window. "What are you doing here?"

"I asked Sara to give you a shout before you left the ground today," Tel said. "She didn't catch you, though. Benny wanted me to ask you about Saturday. Leyton Orient away. D'you reckon there's any chance at all of you playing?"

"Not really," Luke replied, shaking his head. "My stepdad's still working on my mum about the Paris game. But on Saturday she wants the whole family to go house-hunting." He pulled a face. Every now and then his mum decided she needed a bigger garden. So then the three of them had to go tramping round horrible semi-detached houses, measuring up their lawns.

"Ah well, can't be helped," shrugged Terry. "Those three points at Hartlepool last night did us a power of good though. Another couple of wins and we're safe in the league, I reckon. But we do need you for that PSG second leg, Luke. Without you over there, son, it'll be a real PSG – Pointless Second Game."

Luke closed his eyes. His fate was entirely in Rodney's hands. *Could* his stepdad swing it with Luke's mum? To be perfectly frank, Luke doubted it.

"Dog's back to his wicked best, though," Cool F remarked.

"Ooh, what a scorcher he had last night!" drooled Tel. "On song, or what?!"

"So is he going to be playing in Paris?" asked Luke. "I mean, you'd have to get him across the Channel, wouldn't you? What *is* going on, Terry? Tell us. How did you get the Dog to cross the Channel when you came back from Russia?"

Terry looked up at the two boys with the strangest expression. Then he glanced back over his shoulder. Several cars were drawing up behind him. "Oh, here we go," he sighed. "Here comes the press pack. Everywhere I flippin' well go I've got this lot sniffing around behind me, panting for soundbites. Look, lads, hop in the motor. I'll give you both a lift up to Frederick's place. Chop, chop."

"And you'll tell us how you got Dog here from Russia?" said Luke.

"Yeah, yeah, if you like. I've gotta let somebody in on this thing some time. It might as well be you two. But not a word to *anyone* else, mind."

"Brownies' honour," said Cool F as they both piled into the back of the car.

And so at last, as Terry drove the boys across town, he spilled the beans on his mysterious trip back from Moscow with the Dog: "To tell the truth, chaps, I didn't know *what* to do once we'd ridden our tandem as far the French coast. Calais, it was. We got there at night, so Dog didn't see any sea. We put up our tent for the night near the ferry. Then it came to me: knock-out pills!"

"Knock-out pills?" said Luke and Frederick.

"*Monster* knock-out pills. I'd had 'em in my first-aid box for ages. They used to use them to stun big animals at London Zoo – elephants, like – before they was made illegal. The pills, that is, not the elephants." The boys nodded. "Anyway, I got Dog to take a couple before going to sleep. Mimed to him that they were full of vitamins. Went out like a light, he did. Then all I had to do was take down our tent, lug him on board the ferry – and Bob was your uncle." He paused. "Well, actually, that *wasn't* too straightforward. He's a big lad, the Dog. But I managed it. He slept like a baby all the way across to Dover. Then when we got there, I put up the tent again. And when he woke up – he didn't have a clue that he'd moved an inch since he first fell asleep. Presto!"

"Wow," breathed Luke. "Now I see why you didn't want Dog to know Britain is an island. He doesn't actually *know* he's travelled across water?"

"No way. He thinks Britain's joined on to Europe."

"And that's why he's been feeling so rough?" Luke went on. "Side-effects from the pills?"

"Yeah," admitted Terry. "I hadn't bargained for that. But that's all water under Stamford Bridge. Now he's as right as rain, as he showed everyone last night."

"But you can't use the same scam for the Paris trip," Frederick pointed out. "It'll be Side-Effect City all over again."

"Aha! That's where Plan B comes into operation!"

"Plan B?"

"Think *Pedalo*! We're gonna cross the Channel – I'll mime to Dog that it's just a very wide river – but all under our own steam! A twin-seater pedalo. Part of his own personal health-and-fitness programme. I'll tell him that in sign lingo."

Luke and Frederick looked at each other. They didn't say a word. They didn't have to. The words "disaster" and "this will end in" were written as plain as day on both their faces. "You and Dog are going to *pedal* a little wooden boat across the English Channel?" gasped Luke.

"You just watch us!" laughed Terry, pulling up outside Frederick's house. "Although, as a matter of fact, you won't be able to watch us. We're going at night. That way, we'll be able to avoid those blinking media vultures."

Luke's jaw dropped. "You're going to pedal across the Channel in the dark?"

"Trust me," grinned Tel, turning to open the rear door. "I used to be in the Sea Scouts. Well, till I was chucked out. Off you go now, lads. And remember – not a word to a soul! Only Benny, me and Ruel are in on this. And whatever you do – don't let the Dog know he's on an island here. Right?"

"Mum's the word," said Luke, too stunned to say any more.

"As long as it's not *your* mum, eh?" said Tel, before driving off. "But do try and get her to give you the green light for Paris. We need you, Luke!"

14

Saturday afternoon was as dull as any Saturday afternoon Luke had ever spent.

And that was really saying something. For years, before he started playing for Albion, he'd used to watch them on Saturday afternoons. Those were the bad old days. People in the crowd yearned to be at home watching paint drying. But being shown around fourteen houses by seven different estate agents was worse. Even Luke's mum seemed stiff with boredom by the end. Not one of the gardens had been remotely big enough for her. Mission unaccomplished.

When they got back home, there was a message for Rodney on the answer-machine from "Mr Mallard". That snapped Luke out of his stupor. Mr Mallard was Rod's code-name for Benny Webb. (Rod was a mad-keen bird-spotter. In his mind "Webb" led to "Webbed Feet" to "Duck" and then to "Mallard".) "I'll take it upstairs, dear," Rodney said. "It'll only be a boring work conversation."

"Take it where you like," grunted Luke's mum. "Oh, make me some tea, Luke, will you? I haven't got the strength left to lift a tea-bag."

Rod was on the phone a long while. Luke was itching to know what Benny wanted. He also longed to know how Albion had done at Leyton Orient. But he didn't get to speak in private with Rodney till two hours later, when his mum was up in the bath. "Benny basically just wanted to know how my Paris plans were coming on," Rod whispered (even though they were both down in the kitchen).

"And what did you tell him?"

Rodney nodded and winked, but it didn't look convincing. "It's all in hand, trust me. All I've got to do is *get* you to Paris. From that point, TAFKAG takes over. I spoke to him yesterday on the phone from Albania. Or was it Slovenia?"

"But *how* are you going to get me to Paris?" Luke pleaded.

Again Rodney winked. "All will be revealed tomorrow. Over Sunday lunch."

Luke sighed but left it there. "And how about the game? What was the score?"

"One-nil to the Albion! Jimbo was still abroad. Dog scored another cracker!"

"*Brilliant!* Maybe old Mrs Plunkett really did do some good, after all."

"Oh, I'm not so sure about that," Rodney whispered back. "Benny told me what happened after training on Thursday – you know, when the players were meant to go and talk to her and get on the correct spiritual plane? Well, it was a bit of a fiasco. Only Dennis and Chrissie went. Dennis got the wrong end of the stick, as usual. He asked her to put him in touch with the spirit of his dead Grandma. And Chrissie tried to get her to faith-heal a love-bite on his neck."

Luke grinned. Then his mum yelled down for Rodney to come at once and hold the towel for her while she got out of the bath.

The hours crawled by till Sunday lunch. Quite a lot of hours. Luke's mum wasn't the world's speediest cook. She finally got steak-and-kidney pies, oven chips and warm baked beans on to the table by two-thirty in the afternoon. Unless she'd actually been slaughtering a cow in the kitchen for the steak, Luke couldn't guess why it had taken so long. Tinned fruit and ice-cream followed.

"Delicious!" Rodney exclaimed as he put down his spoon. "My congratulations to the chef!" He gave Luke's mum a peck on the cheek – just like one of his beloved bantam cocks. "You really deserve a reward for slaving away for us like that," he went on. "So what would you say to dining out in style for a couple of days next week – at *French* restaurants?"

"Oh, don't be so silly, Rodney," she scowled. "There aren't any French restaurants in town.

Just those pricey *Pret A Manger* sandwich bars."

"Aha!" cried Rodney, twinkling away behind his glasses (though under the table Luke saw his knees trembling). "But these restaurants would be – in France!"

"What *is* all this about France?" she spat. "You've been dropping hints for days. And to be quite honest, Rodney, it's getting on my nerves."

"Fret no more, my dear!" Rod beamed, reaching into the inside pocket of his jacket. (He always wore a jacket and tie for Sunday lunch. He was like that.) "I've splashed out a little – and why not!" He produced a wad of tickets and held them up. "We're going on a romantic mini-break! Tuesday to Thursday! To gay Paree! The city of love. I've booked the flights, the hotel, the *restaurant tables* – the lot!"

"Are you mad?" asked Luke's mum, narrowing her eyes.

"Maybe!" grinned Rodney, his knees knocking now. "Mad for you! I just couldn't resist this." He raised an eyebrow. "It is, after all, our anniversary."

That stumped Luke's mum. It baffled Luke too. "Anniversary?" they both said.

"Yes, dear," Rodney battled on. "The seventh anniversary of the first time we saw a kingfisher together!"

"You *are* mad," she growled. "And anyway, what about Luke? We can't just leave him here."

Rodney fanned out the tickets. "But Luke's coming too! He's included!"

"On a romantic mini-break?" she snorted. Luke shut his eyes. This was nuts. "But he's got school."

"No, no," Rod insisted. "We go straight after school on Tuesday. Then Wednesday's a teacher training day..." (It wasn't, but Luke's mum wasn't to know.) "So he'll only miss Thursday, and I've squared that with his head."

"You've thought of everything, haven't you?" she said, eyeing him with *extreme* suspicion. (Oh no, thought Luke. She's not going to buy it. And if he had been her, he wouldn't have bought it either. *Kingfisher* anniversary! Meanwhile Rod was shaking so much, the cutlery on the table was dancing.) There was a long, awful pause. Then she gave her verdict: "But if you've already paid in advance, well, I suppose we've got to do it."

"Oh, *yippee*!" yelled Rod, collapsing with relief – and dropping all the tickets.

15

When Luke came out of school on Thursday afternoon, his mum and Rodney were waiting outside in the Escort. Unfortunately, so were about a dozen reporters. Doubtless they wanted to know why Luke hadn't left England with Benny and the boys earlier that day. Or where Terry and the Dog were.

As soon as they saw him, their pencils and microphones started to bristle. Nightmare scenario! If his mum saw them approach him, all her old suspicions would kick in again – then he could forget about France. He had to think fast.

"Pssst!" he hissed at the nearest reporter, a woman from the *Daily Mail*. Eagerly she craned her long neck towards him. Then Luke, still walking towards the Escort, said out of the side of his mouth, "Can't stop now. Plane's waiting. But you might just catch Dog and Tel ... at the *Eurostar* Terminal."

"*Eurostar!*" Her eyes lit up as she stashed

her pencil back behind her ear. "Cheers, Luke!" Then off she dashed to her car – followed, after a split second, by all her other media cronies. If she had a scoop, *they* all wanted to be in on it too. So by the time Luke opened the Escort's rear door, the coast was clear.

But you wouldn't have thought so from Luke's mum's attitude. All the way to Heathrow, she banged on about how "inconvenient" this mini-break was. She never quite explained why. Maybe it was all the cups of coffee with Aunt Evelyn that she'd be missing. Or the chances of seeing Des Lynam on an advert.

She didn't perk up much at the airport – especially when their flight was delayed by a cool seventy minutes. "We could have *swum* there by now," she said at around seven-fifteen. Luke suddenly had a worried vision of Dog and Tel pedalling away through the black night. They must have set out the night before – mustn't they? Just how long was a journey like that going to take?

Once they were airborne, his mum's mood took a turn for the worse. She hated the Air France food, they didn't have the sherry she liked on the trolley, and she couldn't get a set of headphones that worked.

"Never mind, dear," Rodney soothed her. "Let me read to you from the guidebook about these lovely parks and gardens we're going to see. Listen to this: '*Approaching the* Auteuil Garden *from the* Garden of the Poets, *you pass the delightful potting sheds with rickety wooden blinds. Then you come into a garden beautifully laid out around big old-fashioned metal-frame greenhouses. There may be a special exhibition of azaleas on in April...*' Doesn't *that* tickle your fancy? And then, just nearby, there's another one. The Albert Kahn Gardens. Listen: '*It's an enchanting place, with rhododendrons and camellias under blue cedars, a rose garden and an orchard, a forest of Moroccan pines and streams with Japanese bridges beside pagoda tea houses...*' I don't know about you. *I* can hardly wait!"

"So our hotel is near these parks, is it?" asked Luke's mum grumpily.

"Yes!" Rodney cried. "I'm sure it will be. I asked the travel agent for somewhere near a park. And all the parks are in the west ... I think. That's the posh part."

A few minutes later Luke picked up the guidebook himself. He found the parks that Rodney had been going on about. True enough, they were in the west. And slap bang nearby was the most important park of all – the Parc des Princes, home of PSG. But he noticed other parks in the east. *Not* in the posh part...

And, of course, when they arrived and gave the taxi-driver the hotel's address, he said that it was in Belleville – way out east. "Belleville – that means pretty town!" said Rodney as they swished away through the heavy evening rain. You could have fooled Luke's mum when they got there. It was hard to get a proper idea of the place in the dark and the rain, but it didn't look promising.

The streets were narrow and the houses badly run-down. But at least the people who lived in them had roofs over their heads. The homeless beggars on every corner just had to get soaked to the skin in the downpour. *Some* of them looked French. Many more were African, or looked a bit like Dog (after his elephant knock-out pills). It didn't really feel like France at all. And most of the restaurants they saw were Chinese or Greek.

"Where's the – er – park?" Rodney asked as they juddered to a halt outside a tall, thin building with the "O" missing from its neon "HOTEL" sign.

The driver jerked a thumb back over his shoulder. "Parç des Buttes-Chaumont," he yawned. "Is small ... but very nice. There's a lake in it. With bridge. Bridge of Suicides, they call it..."

"Yes, yes," Rodney cut in quickly, offering him a wad of French banknotes, "that all sounds *extremely* interesting. Thank you very much, thank you..."

"Bridge of *Suicides*?" Luke's mum repeated all the way into the hotel's dingy foyer. She trod on the carpet as if she thought she might catch a disease from it. To be fair, it didn't look too clean. Nor did the guy wearing an eye-patch standing behind the desk.

And yes, there was a problem. It took the pirate lookalike a long while to explain it to Rodney, who spoke very little French. The French guy was annoyed by that. Once or twice he really seemed about to lose his temper. Then Rodney got the picture. Picking up a key, he came across to where Luke and his mum had sat down on a bench to wait.

"No sweat really," he announced with a fixed and – frankly – sweaty grin. "They've double-booked our rooms. But they've given us another one."

"One?" gasped Luke's mum.

"They're putting a fold-up bed in with us for Luke. Come on – let's climb the stairs. The lift, unfortunately, is out of order…"

They were on the top floor. "The good news," declared Rodney, on leading the way into a room half the size of Luke's bedroom at home, "is that we have our own toilet and washing facilities. That isn't always the case in French hotels."

The bad news, however, as Luke could tell from one sniff, was that the toilet was blocked.

They got a man to come up and look at it. But that's just about all he did do. In the end Luke's mum simply climbed into her bed, still fully clothed, and muttered and mumbled under the blankets until she fell asleep.

Rodney glanced at Luke, who was sitting very close by on his fold-up bed, flicking through the guidebook. "Well," said his ever-optimistic stepdad, "it's not what I had in mind, I must admit. But it could be worse."

Luke could only nod back.

Then he looked again at the guidebook. Their hotel was in it. *Perfectly located*, it said, f*or anyone passionate about the nearby Père Lachaise cemetery*.

Yep, thought the Studless Sensation, that just about sums it up.

16

It took Luke and Rodney ages to get off to sleep. Until about three a.m. there seemed to be a street party going on outside. Then the police sirens started. Luke's mum slept through it all. But a good night's sleep didn't make her any sweeter. Angrily she shook Luke and Rodney awake at nine-thirty. "If we don't go down for breakfast soon," she moaned, "there will be no food left!"

As it happened, there was plenty of food down in the hotel restaurant. The three of them stood behind a locked glass door and watched it all being stashed away for the day. Apparently breakfast finished at nine-fifteen on the dot. Mr Eyepatch wouldn't even let them have a couple of croissants to take up to their room.

"Why on earth didn't you ask *last night* what time breakfast was?" Luke's mum ranted at Rodney. "It's bad enough to *be* in this vile place!! But to be in here and starving to death – ohhhhh!!!" She stamped her foot in fury.

"There, there, dear," said Rodney, staring down into the street from the small window. "We'll find a nice café to eat in. And look, I'm sure the rain's easing off a bit now. Soon we'll be strolling through those gardens. I've got a feeling that something really special is going to happen here. Something ... magical."

Just as he spoke, an enormous thunderclap sounded outside. Then a flash of lightning. Luke could see from his bed that the rain was sheeting down as hard as ever. This wasn't going well. Apart from anything else, he was meant to be at the Parc des Princes in half an hour – for a training session with the rest of the squad. The night before, Rodney had sworn to him that he would get there. But when Luke asked how, he'd just winked.

"Well, I'm going to take a shower," Luke's mum barked. "No doubt there won't be any hot water. But I feel so *filthy* after all that travelling yesterday."

Moments after she shut herself into the bathroom, there was a knock at the outer door.

"If they've decided to send us some breakfast after all," she shouted over the sound of rushing water, "tell them we're not interested. That man was *so* rude!"

But as Rodney went across to the door, he winked again at Luke. What *was* this?

"Hey there!" cried a delighted voice from out

in the corridor when Rodney opened up. "Nice pad you've got here! Groovy district too. Ghetto-blasters everywhere on the streets, man. Kids rapping on all the corners. *Way* funky!"

"Dad!" Luke gasped, glancing at the bathroom door. Was this part of Rodney's plan to get him to training? He went on in a whisper: "What are y*ou* doing here?"

"Lukey baby!" he cried back, taking one step into the room – which suddenly became a lot brighter, thanks to his neon-yellow flared trousers and the orange polka-dot bandanna on his head. "How's it hangin', dude?"

"*Is that who I think it is?!*" yelled Luke's mum from under her shower.

"Er ... yes, dear," Rodney answered quickly. He was looking at Luke a bit oddly, then glancing back out into the corridor, as if someone else was out there too. "As luck would have it, Luke's dad is over here in Paris for a gig tonight. He's volunteered to take Luke off for the day – so that you and I can have some – um – quality romantic time together. He'll bring him back after the concert. OK?"

Suddenly the sound of gushing water stopped. The two men and Luke stood staring wide-eyed at each other, all with their fingers crossed. They even tilted their heads towards the bathroom door, as if to overhear what she was thinking. *Quality romantic time*, Luke himself was thinking, *with my mum!*

Just as suddenly as before, the shower blasted back on again. "All right," she roared above the racket. "But Luke's got to be back here by midnight. This is still a school day as far as he's concerned. He can't stay up all hours!"

The three guys gazed at one another. What had come over her? She just kept on being almost normal. It was amazing.

"Let's hit the road then, dude," TAFKAG said quickly – before she could have any second thoughts. "Got all your stuff? Let's go see what's cooking in this mega-special city." As he said the last bit, he pretended to be kicking a football, so that Luke knew exactly where he'd be taking him.

"I'm ready," Luke grinned, but he saw Rodney was still glancing into the corridor.

"And hey," cried TAFKAG, "you'll never believe this – but I've brought someone *else* along. Someone who's trucked all the way to Paris, France just to get a load of you! She got her dad to bring her specially – and there she was last night, staying in the same hotel as me! I didn't realize you were a babe-magnet, Lukey! And from what she tells me, you'll be over the moon to get it together with her again. Come and see who I've got waiting for you outside."

Luke gulped, then felt his dad's arm around

his shoulder, guiding him out of the room. He couldn't feel his feet on the floor at all. This was impossible. Surely it couldn't be *her*? Surely he was still asleep and this was just a nightmare? He closed his eyes as he left the room. He didn't dare look to the right.

"Oh, Lu-u-uke," purred an all-too-familiar German voice.

Uschi. *USCHI!*

That word she'd been mouthing at Heathrow, it was "Paris"! And from the way she was fluttering her eyelashes at him, this time it was *really* personal.

17

Uschi didn't say another word until they climbed into TAFKAG's van outside.

She'd lurched forward to greet him with a kiss, but Luke reached out fast and shook her hand instead. Then quickly he led the way down the stairs and out into the teeming rain. There wasn't enough room for them both in the front of the van. So Luke climbed in the back with all the amps and speakers.

"Okey-dokey!" cried TAFKAG, revving up and scattering a gang of sodden urchins who were about to nick his hub-caps. "It's off to the Parc des Princes!"

Luke's heart then sank even further as his dad passed Uschi a big street-map of the city. It took him yonks to find where they were, then yonks longer to spot where they were going. And all the while, Uschi kept looking back at Luke over her shoulder, fluttering away like it was going out of fashion. He did his best to smile back in a way that didn't encourage her too much. But again and again, those words of hers came back to haunt him: *Ah Paris, the city of romance*... This crazy German girlie really thought they had a "lurve thang" going now!

TAFKAG made a horrible hash of getting to the stadium. In England he wasn't the best (or smoothest) of drivers. Over here, he was the pits. Luke lost count of the number of times he toppled over as his dad pulled up sharp when blasts from other cars' horns told him he was on the wrong side of the road – or driving in the wrong direction up a one-way street.

Uschi wasn't much good as a navigator, either. All that eyelash-fluttering probably stopped her from seeing the map properly. In the end, Luke took it from her, and although reading it make him feel sicker than ever, he did manage to get them to their destination: the soaring 49,000-capacity Parc des Princes at twenty-four Rue du Commandant Guilbaud – headquarters of France's fabulous international rugby union team as well as the football home of PSG.

"There you go then, sunshine," sighed TAFKAG, shaking his ponytail. "Sorry about the slight delay. But hey, get out on that pitch and sock it to 'em, baby! We'll come in and watch when I've parked up this old banger."

Luke managed to stagger down on to the tarmac without having to kiss Uschi goodbye.

As the van juddered off, he took a dizzy look at his watch. Eleven-fifteen. He was an hour and a quarter late. Benny was not going to be chuffed. In fact, wasn't that the old boy himself – over there in that doorway, waving?

"Luke, son!" Benny shouted, waving harder. "Don't just stand there getting soaked! Get yourself inside. Where've you *been*, son? We've nearly finished."

Luke took a deep breath, then trotted in a fairly straight line towards his manager. "Sorry, Boss," he gasped. "Bit of trouble getting here."

"But you're going to be all right for tomorrow night, right?" asked Benny, guiding him inside the great big bowl of a stadium, and down the first corridor.

"Er ... well, yes, I think so," Luke said. "Rodney must have some sort of plan."

"I hope to high heaven he has," Benny grunted, pushing back the door to the empty dressing-room and holding it open for Luke to enter. "As things stand, we're woefully short of numbers. Terry and Dog haven't shown up yet – and frankly I'm worried about that. Between you and me, I was never too keen on that pedalo business. Seemed seriously iffy from the start."

"But everyone else is here?" Luke asked, pulling off his sweatshirt and plucking the Number Seven training shirt off its peg.

Benny sat down heavily on the bench opposite before answering. He didn't look thrilled. There even seemed to be a sag to his sheepskin coat.

"Well," he sighed, "in a manner of speaking, everyone else *is* here. Here in Paris, I mean. But Dennis and Craig are off on a working breakfast – whatever that is – with a French publisher. Madman's off filming a sketch for his chat show at the Eiffel Tower. Then Carl is doing an advert for the French Pineapple Marketing Board. And now Chrissie is having talks with some bunch of perfume-makers about a new fragrance for men – although to be honest, even if he was here he wouldn't be much use. He's so head-over-heels in love with our work experience girl, he spends more time looking at her than at the ball!"

Luke finished pulling on his kit, then slipped back into his trainers. He hardly dared ask his next question. "And Jimbo? Is he – er – fit to play tomorrow?"

Benny closed his eyes and ran a despairing hand over his beard. Even though no one else was in the room, he looked around before replying. "If you mean 'Has anyone managed to nobble him in training this morning?' I'm afraid the answer is no. He wasn't takin' any chances. He didn't even get changed – just in case his injury jinx hit again. And he's brought along that ... *woman* too. She's out there on the pitch with the squad now."

"On the pitch?" asked Luke, picturing Mrs Plunkett in boots and a training bib.

"Jimbo's put her on call for the players twenty-four hours a day." Benny gritted his teeth. "So if – say – Narris isn't tackling the plastic cones viciously enough, he can go over and talk to her, and see if he's got a deep psychological problem." His face went purple, then he threw back his great head, opened his mouth and let out a bone-shaking roar. "*Oh, how did it ever get to be like this?* The eve of the biggest game in Albion's history and we've lost the plot, Luke! I can't *believe* we're letting all this extra-terrestrial nonsense ruin our preparations!"

"Extra-mural," came a small male voice from nowhere.

"Sorry?" said Benny, glancing around in what looked like panic.

"The word is extra-*mural*," the voice repeated – and it was coming from beyond the wall to the shower area. "You've made this mistake before, Mr Webb. It means other activities. Extra-*terrestrial* means something from outer space."

While the voice gave this explanation Benny slowly, softly stepped across to where it was coming from. Now Luke could see an old-fashioned cine-camera lens poking around the wall's end. It was the fly-on-the-wall team!

"*You!*" Benny bellowed, striding out in front

of the lens. He seemed to swell up to twice his normal size. "Now *that* is as much as I can take for one day!" Then he seized the camera, ripped it open, and started tugging out loops and loops of film.

"No, no!" yelled the director, still unseen by Luke. "You never said we couldn't film in *this* dressing-room! Only at Ash Acre! And it's only me in here – not the whole unit. And I'm just recording this for myself! It's a home-movie! *Stop!* Please *stop*!"

But Benny didn't stop. And when he had finished, he tossed away the camera then disappeared from Luke's view, holding the film menacingly in front of him like a length of rope.

Luke thought it was best to disappear too at that point – just as the director began to scream. Out on the pitch, he managed twenty minutes of free-kick practice before the torrents of rain stopped play for the day. And when the Albion lads got back into the dressing-room, an odd sight met them down on the shower-room floor. "What is it?" laughed Half-Fat. "A mummy?"

But no. It was just a TV documentary director, all tied up from head to foot in his own ruined film. "Not so much fly-on-the-wall as guy-on-the-floor," grinned Casper Franks, carefully stepping over him on his way to the toilet.

18

Luke pleaded with Frederick to stay with him, Uschi and TAFKAG for the rest of that day. "Safety in numbers," he explained. Half-Fat, Narris, Gaffer and Darius all tagged along too. "We were just gonna see the sights anyway," they grinned at Luke. "We might as well see them with you and your missis!"

They went right up the Eiffel Tower and right through the Louvre art gallery. They looked over Notre Dame cathedral, they zipped across to see the famous hilltop church at Sacre-Cœur. Then they rounded off the afternoon with a quick dash through the amazing glassy Pompidou Centre of Art and Culture. It seemed to have been built inside out. Even the escalator was on the outside in a long glass tube. Apparently the architects had wanted the entire thing to look like "horizontal streets in the air".

And how did half a dozen footballers and a dippy-hippie musician know this? Because they were informed by the only lady in their party – Fräulein Uschi.

Boy, did she know about Paris! She was like a whole set of encyclopedias on the city. Her dad had business partners there, and he often brought her along on his trips. In fact, he was in top-level meetings all that day. "Yet he shall be free in time to catch your father's concert this evening," Uschi gushed at Luke when they piled into a restaurant for an early dinner, then fluttered at him like fury.

Luke smiled back. He couldn't help it really. The thing was: when he wasn't on his own with her, he really quite *liked* Uschi. She'd been brilliant as a guide that day. She'd even chased away a pack of unwelcome paparazzi on the Rue de Rivoli. And – as she now showed while everyone piled into their steak and French fries – she knew her football too. *Plus* she had a sense of humour.

"I am afraid," she grinned, "that you must find someone else to fall on top of Mr Jimbo Prince before tomorrow's game. When he glimpsed me at the stadium today, he turned and ran as if I had been a gang of Millwall fans!"

"You're right, Uschi," nodded Half-Fat. "We do indeed need somebody to drop from a very great height on top of our useless player-chairman."

"We've had it if he plays," Narris agreed. "I really wish he'd just buzz off. I know he saved the club and everything last year. But as far as I'm concerned, he can keep his money now. I don't even like that new ground of his! To me, it's just creepy. All those shiny plastic seats. No rusting metal. Ugh!" He screwed up his face at the pain of it all. "And where the flip's Dog, too?"

"Search me," said Gaffer. "Him and Tel could be anywhere now. But Benny doesn't reckon it's a *Titanic* job. Neil Veal's not in Paris yet, either. Benny thinks he must have arranged some publicity stunts up on the coast."

Everyone fell silent, thinking of the uphill struggle ahead. Then TAFKAG snapped his fingers and grooved to his feet. "Hey, guys, I've got just the thing to blow away your pre-match blues!" He tossed down a fistful of complimentary tickets for that night's gig at the La Petite Banane – a hot new club right on the river Seine. "Just me, an acoustic guitar and a whole lot of happening vibes! I'll even take you in my van! Come on – I'm late for my soundcheck."

None of the four grown-up players had the heart to turn him down. He was, after all, Castle Albion's official pop star – more or less. Luke and Uschi already had tickets, of course. And Frederick was going to be putting in a guest rap appearance, just as he had on the FA Cup Final single. So off they all dashed through the rain to the TAFKAG-mobile. Then off they all lurched to the river.

On the way (and thanks to his dad's dodgy driving, it was quite a long way), Luke kept wondering what sort of a day Rodney and his mum were having. The rain hadn't stopped for a minute. Strolling through parks simply wasn't on. And his mum didn't really like doing anything else – except looking out for Des Lynam on television, and they didn't have ITV in Paris. Ho hum.

Finally they arrived at La Petite Banane. How did Neil Veal find these places to book TAFKAG into? When he'd said it was "right on the river Seine", he wasn't kidding. It wasn't a building but a barge. A big, Chinese-looking thing tied up to the quay near the National Library. But it *was* a music club, and people in black suits and ties *were* trooping up the gangplank and inside.

"Looks a bit posh, don't it?" said Darius, stooping down and trying to rub some of the dirt off his trainers. "You sure this is the right place?"

"Right enough," said Cool F, nodding at a poster wrapped round a nearby lamp-post. "*Here – tonight, England's hip dude TAFKAG – Sixties Style Songs like you've never heard them before!*" He turned to Luke's dad and gave him a quick, complicated handshake. "Hey, England's TAFKAG – big up!"

Once inside, they met up with Uschi's dad, and TAFKAG did a quick sound-check. He just strummed through a song from his soon-to-be-released album. The English party tried not to wince at the obviously heart-felt chorus:

"*Let's swim with the dolphins*
And sing with the whales,
Let's lay a load of groovy peace
On everything with tails."

But to their amazement, by the end of the song the French punters at the other tables were all singing along. With completely straight faces! And although they were dressed like penguins, they clapped like penguins too. Not just for the soundcheck, but for every single number TAFKAG "laid on them" afterwards.

There was no accounting for national taste. As Luke's dad ploughed through his bizarre backwards-version of the Beatles' "Strawberry Fields Forever" (or "Forever Fields Strawberry", as he introduced it), they even started swaying in their seats! And when Frederick climbed onstage for a killer rap during *Daytrip to the Donkey Sanctuary Blues*, they danced! In a very serious way, of course.

The whole thing went *way* better than any gig that Luke had seen his dad do at home. Maybe he really was on the road to international fame and riches now. Uschi certainly thought so. She'd been sitting safely opposite

Luke all night. But during the fourth encore – *Almost Trimmed My Ponytail (Just The Other Day)* – with everyone now on their feet, she suddenly popped up next to him.

"*Ach* Luke," she purred in his ear, "this is so fantastic! To be in Paris – the centre of the romantic universe! To be in La Petite Banane in such fine company and hearing such beautiful music! And above all else, to be in lo-o-ove..."

Taking fright, Luke looked at her and saw she was puckering up her lips. "Just one kiss, Studless," she said swoonily, grabbing his arm hard as his dad soared towards *Ponytail*'s final chorus, "this is all I request to make my joy complete. One kiss, to show that underneath we both feel the same way..."

But just when Luke thought his number was up, TAFKAG's number *was*. He was always snapping the odd string on stage. But this time, in striking all six with a mid-air windmill swing of his arm, he broke the lot!

The audience thought he'd done it on purpose, to show that nothing lasts in life, even ponytails. At once they broke into a barge-rocking storm of applause. And Uschi had to let Luke go to join in. But, wow – another narrow escape, or what?

19

Luke got back to the hotel just as midnight struck. Rodney was waiting for him nervously down in the foyer. "Thank heavens you're back safely!" he cried, as they headed straight upstairs together. "I don't think your mum could face another crisis today."

"*Another* one?" asked Luke.

Rodney paused to get his breath and buff his glasses. "She had one of her worst-ever headaches this morning – after we got soaked trying to find the parks. But she recovered in time for a romantic candle-lit dinner ... and then got food-poisoning. The doctor's just left. Don't make any loud noises in the room, eh?"

As it turned out, Luke could have made as much noise as he liked. His mum moaned so much until dawn that she wouldn't have heard anyway. But by the time Luke and Rodney slipped downstairs for breakfast, she was sound asleep.

"Look," said Rodney over the slightly stale

bread and lukewarm coffee, "she's going to be out of it all morning now. You can nip off to training at the stadium again. Just get back in time for lunch. And oh, what do you think about that, then?" He pointed to the French sports newspaper that the man at the next table was reading. "It looks as if our lost Dog's been found as well."

Luke glanced across and saw a big photo of Superdog snipping the ribbon to open a new French hypermarket. Behind him stood a grinning Neil Veal – and an anxious Terry V looking at his watch. But they were all in one piece. And Dog didn't look in the least bit dazed. Pedalos rule OK, thought Luke.

"Cheers, Rodney," he grinned. "I could do with a decent training session before tonight. I think we all could. But … I *will* be able to play tonight, right?"

Rodney nodded then narrowed his eyes behind his specs. His grip on his coffee cup tightened. "Trust me, Luke," he said with a quivering lip. "I *do* have a feeling that something special is going to happen here. Something … magical."

"Like us getting through to the final?" beamed Luke.

"Stranger things have happened at sea," said Rodney, pointing again at pedalo-Dog's newspaper photo before getting up to call Luke a taxi and seeing him off.

When Luke arrived at the Parc des Princes this time, there was a whole new feel to the squad. For a start, everyone was present and correct. Even Jimbo was out on the pitch – although again he chose not to do any actual training. ("I just can't risk it," Luke overheard him telling a po-faced Benny. "This is *such* a big game tonight. You wouldn't want me to go and crock myself, would you?") But they weren't there only for the photo-opportunity – which a huge crowd of Europe's top sports-snappers had come for. When all the team pics and player portraits had been shot, Benny put his lads through *such* a training session.

Luke had never seen his team-mates lap a pitch faster or more often. Never heard fewer complaints as the boss had them dribbling around cones for almost half an hour. Never imagined that so many set-piece rehearsals could go *exactly* to plan – again and again and again. Pumping away in that pedalo had obviously done Dog a power of good. His dead-ball work was awesomely accurate, his sprinting in a league of its own. He'd even picked up another English word. Whenever anyone complimented him on his sublime skills, he would reply with a dazzling toothy grin: "I am exceedingly *delighted* to meet you!"

Meanwhile Chrissie was back to his best. His whole focus was now on football – except when he scored with a particularly brilliant scissors-kick from a Luke corner, and, just briefly, blushed at his beloved Sara Briar up in the empty stand.

Madman looked more agile than at any point that season, Gaffer more dominant in the air, Narris and Half-Fat more mobile on the deck, Dennis and Craig more confident in possession, Carl more likely to hit the target than his usual ratio of once in every five shots. It was as if every single one of them had eaten *at least* three Weetabixes for breakfast.

Then Benny rounded off the morning with a full-scale practice match. On one side was the starting line-up for that night – but with Number Twelve Narris in for the uninvolved Jimbo. On the other side were the rest of the subs, plus the Centre of Excellence boys that Ruel had brought over for the experience.

Talk about a corker! That fifteen-minute-each-way clash turned out to be a footie masterclass. It wasn't just that the first-choice team played out of their skins. The other lot were fantastic too. Casper, Keats and Darius turned it on like never before – all three scoring blinding goals. But still they couldn't hope to match Luke and Frederick, who, with two goals apiece, wrapped up a famous victory.

When Benny blew for full-time, a small cheer went up from where the ITV lads were setting up their cameras. The players looked, grinned, then bowed graciously to accept the TV guys' applause. "Hey," said Chrissie, "that's Ron Atkinson giving us the thumbs-up, isn't it?"

"Yeah," cried Casper. "And look who's clapping next to him: Des Lynam!"

Luke blinked. There he was. *Him*. In the flesh. Des, Des, Des! The slickest smoothie in soccer-presenting. "If only my mum knew what she was missing!" he murmured to Cool F, who knew all about her obsession with Mr Des Lynam.

As each player left the pitch, Benny gave him a solemn pat on the back. "If we play like that tonight," said Half-Fat to the boss, "we'll murder them, right?"

"Yeah, but tonight it's not just *us* who will be playing, is it?" muttered Dennis. Several of the others looked where he was looking – across the pitch at Jimbo, who was deep in conversation with Mrs Plunkett. Their shoulders drooped.

"Oh, how did we ever get in this mess with Princey?" wailed Carl. "Can't we hire a hit-man or something? Just take out that prat once and for all?"

Luke glanced at Benny. So did all the others – expecting him to defend the useless player-chairman as usual. But this time he didn't. Instead he nodded his big grey head, just once.

Then he thoughtfully stroked his beard. "I hear you," he said in a strange voice. "And to be fair, I can't disagree with you. What we need here is a Gordian Knot solution." Then he strode off to join Tel and Ruel.

"Gordon who?" asked Keatsy.

"Gord-*i*-an," Frederick corrected him. "History. There was once this wicked great knot at a place called Gordium. Dudes said: whoever undoes it will be master of all Asia. Alexander the Great hits town. Takes one look, draws his sword, and *cuts* right through the rope. No more knot!"

"And did he become master of all Asia afterwards?" asked Chrissie.

Fred nodded.

"But what's that got to do with us tonight?" asked Madman. "The UEFA Cup's only for European teams, ain't it?"

"Benny's obviously got something up his sleeve," said Gaffer with a shrug. "Some sort of sudden-death solution to the Jimbo problem?"

"Maybe he really *is* gonna hire a hit-man!" murmured Carl in awe.

"From the look on his face over there," Gaffer replied, "you could be right."

20

When Luke got back to the hotel, Rodney was again waiting in the foyer. So was TAFKAG. And … Uschi. His dad high-fived him, while Uschi presented a cheek but Luke just shook her hand, then took a brisk step back.

"I rang your dad at his hotel—" Rodney began to explain.

"And I noticed your father departing," Uschi added with a flutter, "so I asked if I might accompany him – if he was coming to see…" her voice dropped to a throaty, passionate sigh, "…*you*."

"The thing is," Rodney went on, "your mum's still pretty wobbly upstairs, but I think she's on the mend now. She'll be catching up on her sleep for most of this afternoon. Then maybe at last we'll be able to have a romantic evening together tonight – even though that'll mean me missing your big game, Luke. Anyway, just to be on the safe side, I thought *you* should spend the rest of today 'sightseeing' with TAFKAG here.

Your mum's quite happy with that – as long as you're back by midnight again. At least, she didn't throw a fit when I told her." He fought back a smile. "To be honest, she didn't have the strength."

"Oh cheers, Rodney!" grinned Luke. "You've sorted this all out brilliantly!"

"Well, me and your dad between us," Rodney corrected him. "So why don't you three go and grab a bite of lunch now? Then, Luke, you can get yourself psychologically prepared for the match back at your dad's hotel."

Uschi's face lit up at that. Luke knew he would have to make it very clear that he needed to make those vital psychological preparations in private.

"And all I have to do now," Rodney concluded, sounding a bit choked-up, "is wish you – and the rest of the lads – all the luck in the world tonight. As I've said all along, and I'm not often wrong about these things, I sense that something special is about to happen. Something truly ... *magical*."

"Yeah, right," grinned Luke. "I'll be happy if we win by three own goals to nil – just as long as we get through to the final. See you, Rodney!"

TAFKAG, still on Cloud Nine after his triumphant gig, took Luke and Uschi to lunch in a Thai bistro full of hip students. A live Asian jazz band was playing, and everyone was wearing such weird retro gear that Luke's dad looked almost smart in comparison. No chance of him being asked to get changed here!

But after the food, he *was* asked to get up and jam with the band. Word got around fast in Paris. The guys already knew how to play *Almost Trimmed My Ponytail*. All "England's TAFKAG" had to do was add his unique vocals.

And that was just the start. Three hours later they were still going strong. And still the punters couldn't get enough. By six p.m. the place was packed with people who had come right across the city to be there. And when TAFKAG grinned that he had to go, "to deliver my funky young son and heir to the Parc des Princes for a little appointment with PSG", there was almost a riot in protest.

Finally the three of them fought their way out. Then it was just a matter of TAFKAG finding his way to the Parc des Princes through the early-evening traffic. Needless to say, that wasn't exactly a piece of cake. It was almost seven by the time Luke jumped down from the van outside the great throbbing arena.

"Do it, Lukey baby!" TAFKAG shouted down. "You're just one game away from the final now! We wanna be there in Rome, right? Oh, sock it to 'em!"

"I wish you such luck, Luke," Uschi cried out

over his dad's shoulder. "Not that you shall need it, of course. You *are* the Studless Sensation! Tonight you shall prove this to the whole watching world! Do it for yourself. Do it for Albion. Do it for England. And, if I may be so bold, do it for me! No – for *us*!"

"Yeah – OK," smiled Luke, giving her the thumbs-up. Almost at once he was mobbed by French autograph-hunters. He scribbled his name on a few programmes, then with the help of two policemen he broke free and headed for the players' entrance. There was a mega-buzz outside the ground. And it didn't stink *at all* like Ash Acre or any other English stadium. No onions, no burgers. Just some rather delicious wafts of fresh French fries.

Outside the entrance, ITV's Gary Newbon had grabbed hold of David Ginola for a quick interview as he went past. "No disrespect to Castle Albion," Luke heard the sleekly-maned superstar saying, "but I cannot see zem getting a result 'ere tonight. Zey should not 'ave given away three goals at Ash Acre. Zey 'ave done magnificently in zis tournament but 'ere it is zee end of zee road for zem."

Then a hand grabbed the mike and twisted it away from the Frenchman. The hand of Terry Vaudeville! "I could argue with that, David," yelled Tel with a flick of his hair, "but I won't, and d'you know why? *Because you're not worth it!*" And with that, he reached out and put an arm round Luke. "Come on, son. Let's get you inside and changed. Benny's got a bit of news for you all."

Terry hustled Luke past all the stewards, heavies and PSG officials, then down the corridor towards the dressing-room. "What news?" Luke gasped. "It's nothing bad, is it? No last-minute hitches?"

"No, son," grinned Tel, pausing outside the door. "Quite the opposite, I'd say."

Then in they both went – to be greeted by an almighty, EU-sized roar as the juiciest pineapple in the Porte St-Martin market smacked Carl Davey fair and square on the bottom. "Nice hit, Craig," said Dennis, nodding in approval.

"Good to see you, Luke," said Benny, all sheepskinned-up as usual. "Get your kit on quick, son. Then I want you all to pay attention." He looked so *serious*! Maybe – thought Luke as he pulled on his shirt and shorts – he was just fed up that Mrs Plunkett was in the big dressing-room again, over there with Jimbo.

"Up for it, Studless?" asked Ruel, next to Luke.

"No," Narris answered for him. "He'd rather be doing his homework!"

"All right then?" Benny called out, clapping for some hush. "You'd better all sit down for this. I've got something to say to you. All of

117

you. Well, to be strictly accurate, it's only to one of you really..."

"Make your mind up, Boss!" Half-Fat laughed, heading a ball across the room to Chrissie, who headed it firmly back. But Benny didn't smile.

"This isn't easy for me," the Big Guy struggled on, frowning and looking around at each player in turn. "I've been at this club for eleven years now. I've known the bad times and the good, the ups and the downs. But I've never had to make a tougher decision than I've had to make here in France today..."

"Oh no – hold the front page!" cried Madman. "Benny's changed his socks!"

Benny turned two big sad eyes on him. "No, Morty. It's bigger than that."

"Your vest?" suggested Casper in his sub's shirt.

Benny raised both hands. "OK, OK. Have your laugh. But I've really been going through agonies on this one. I've looked at it from every angle. Tried to work out what's best for everyone concerned. But in the end I had to do what's best for the club. Because no player – however big – can be bigger than Castle Albion FC. And no *game* has ever been bigger in Albion's history than this one tonight. It's a once-in-a-lifetime thing. We've got to give it our one hundred per cent best shot. We've *got* to.

So, if I hadn't made this incredibly tough decision, then I don't think I would ever have been able to hold up my head again…"

"Right," said Carl, "so you're leaving the sugar out of our half-time tea, then?"

"No, Carl," Benny said slowly. "I'm leaving Jimbo out of the side."

21

For a moment Luke felt as if he had floated a few feet off the bench. From the looks on the other players' faces, so did they. Benny's bombshell still seemed to be swirling round them all. *I'm leaving Jimbo out of the side*.

Then the brief spell was broken. "You can't!" snorted little Jimbo himself.

"I have to," Benny said back, all apologetic but determined too. "We'll always be in your debt, Mr Prince, for what you've done for the club. As a chairman you're a dream-come-true for all of us. But as a *player*..." He didn't actually go on to use the words "worst nightmare", but what he meant was clear enough.

"I don't think you understand," Jimbo laughed again, his face drained of colour. "You *can't* drop me. I *am* this club. Without me, you don't exist!"

"Yes, as I've said," Benny soldiered on, "we can never be grateful enough to you and your millions, Mr P. You're right. If you hadn't stepped in last May, we would have gone right down the plughole. But chairmen are chairmen and players are players, and the two can never really go together. Not in the same person – if you don't mind me saying so."

Jimbo's jaw quivered. His knees were trembling too. "Well, yes, I *do* mind! And I should imagine that some of my team-mates here mind too! Let me just get this clear. You're saying: *I'm not good enough to be in the side on merit?*"

He let out a mad hoot, then looked round the dressing-room – eyes out on stalks behind his specs. Plainly he expected the other players to leap to his defence. But no one said a word. Everyone looked back at him. But no one spoke.

"I see," he said softly, after an awfully long moment. He squinted at Benny. "You've poisoned all their minds against me? I see." Mrs Plunkett, looking shell-shocked herself, put a hand on his shivering arm. But he didn't want her sympathy, and he just shrugged it off. "I *see*!" he said again, starting to nod.

"I'd put you on the bench," Benny went on, raising both palms helplessly, "but what would be the point? I could never bring you on. Not in such a vital game. You do your best, Jimbo. But we just can't risk you out there. I'm so sorry."

Jimbo looked at him, then his face twisted into the weirdest smile. Luke couldn't tell what spiritual plane he was on at that moment, but he was very glad indeed not to be on it with him. "You're sorry," Jimbo whispered, still smiling, nodding harder. "You're ... sorry." He took a last look round at all the players. For a split-second, Luke felt so sorry too that he almost said something nutty like, "Oh, can't we just fit him in somewhere?" But he didn't. He couldn't.

And then it was too late. Jimbo's eyes burned into Benny. "Well, obviously," he said in a furious, choked-up voice, "this club's not big enough for both of us!"

Benny stared back. If they'd had guns in their belts, the shooting would have started then. But they didn't have guns. Only footballs. And even JP must have known that if he tried to boot a ball at Benny, he had less than a one-in-fifty chance of hitting him. Instead, he did something that stunned everyone.

He walked out. Just like that. Straight across the dressing-room floor, pausing only to call back over his shoulder, "Come on, Doris." But then as he held the door open for her, he threw a murderous look at Benny. "I'll see *you* in my office at the Majestic Stadium. Tomorrow at noon. *Be* there!"

And that was it. Exit Jimbo. The door slammed shut and he was gone.

The dressing-room seemed to hum. For

maybe ten seconds, the only sound was made by players' jaws hitting the floor. Then up jumped Narris – who was now, of course, back in the side. Punching the air, he yelled: "*Ye-s-s-s-sssss!*"

After that, everyone else leapt up, punching, whooping, kissing Benny then hoisting him shoulder-high and doing a lap of honour around the showers. It was hard not to be over the moon. Without Jimbo shooting them in the foot at regular intervals, Albion really did have a chance now. Especially if they played like they had in training that morning. It was brilliant! Magic! T'riffic!

Then, above all the hollering and high-fiving, Benny's voice sounded again. He was still way up high, balancing on the shoulders of Gaffer and Carl. But *what* was he saying? Baffled, the players gazed up at him as if he'd flipped.

"*...And you, good yeomen,*" he was shouting now, both fists clenched, "*Whose limbs were made in England, now show us here the mettle of your pasture...*"

"What's that about pasture?" asked Dennis. "Is this about your sheep, Dog?"

"I am exceedingly delighted to meet you," the Dog replied, shrugging.

"*...I see you stand like greyhounds in the slips,*" Benny roared on, "*Straining upon the start. The game's afoot! Follow your spirit; and* *upon this charge, Cry 'God for Harry, England and Saint George!'*"

"Cry *what*?" asked Madman. "And who's this Harry? Not a new player?"

"It's Shakespeare," Cool F explained with a nod. "*Henry V* – the king's speech to the English squaddies just before the big ruck at Agincourt. What the boss is saying is: Get Out There Now And Do It For England!"

"*Ye-e-e-e-a-a-a-a-h-h-h-h-h-h!*" boomed the entire squad in unison, before charging out to the tunnel all fired up for battle – and letting Big Boss Benny tumble to the dressing-room floor in a sheepskin heap.

22

Luke was so fired up that when he raced out on to the pitch, he felt he could have played against all 49,000 rowdy fans, not just the eleven PSG-men.

But a huge wedge of those fans were wearing blue and white hoops. And they were dreaming and praying just as hard as anyone in the Albion side. As Narris raised his arm to salute them, Luke could almost hear several thousand Albion supporters scratching their heads and asking, "But where's Jimbo?" – before waving back in sheer glee at this sudden, unexpected team-change.

And when the stadium announcer confirmed that Phizzo was definitely in for Princey, Rocky and the Southsiders went completely ape:

"He's Big, He's Bad,
He Plays For Trinidad:
Narris Phiz, Narris Phiz!"

they sang out into the Parisian night air.

Without Jimbo to worry about, all the Albion

players looked as if they felt five stone lighter. Their every touch at the kick-in was crisp and clean. And Madman's handling in goal was as safe as houses, despite the slippery wet ball. At long last now it had stopped raining, but the pitch looked really muddy. It wasn't a night for fancy football. Albion were going to have to get stuck in as if there were no tomorrow. And as far as the UEFA Cup was concerned, there *was* no tomorrow for Albion unless they won this match by three clear goals.

"So just let me run this past you," Carl called to Luke as Gaffer trotted up to the centre-spot for the toss. "If we win here *two*-nil, that won't be any good?"

"Nope," said Luke with a grin. Carl was the world's worst mathematician when it came to working out scores over two legs. "You see, they beat us three-one at our place—"

"Yeah," Carl cut in, as Gaffer won the toss and chose to kick off, "but if we won here two-nil, that would make it three-three altogether, right?"

"Wrong. Away goals count double, remember? PSG would win because they would then have three and we'd have only two." Carl looked back at him blankly, but Luke just laughed and shook him by the arm. "Look, we're going to win by *more* than two-nil! And we can start clocking up the goals right away, by trying that kick-off move we worked out in training today."

Carl winked, pointed to the spot on his shorts where the lucky pineapple had whacked him, and trotted over to the centre-spot. As the crowd cranked up the noise level even higher, and the ref signalled to both his assistants in turn, Dog, Luke and Carl all glanced at one another and nodded.

The Kick-Off Move. Phew. This was going to be a long-shot – literally. The chances of it working were fairly low. But in training they had scored with it five times out of five – and all in that far goal too. It had to be worth a try.

The whistle shrieked and off they went. PSG v Albion, for a place in the UEFA Cup Final in Rome! Dog tapped the ball to Carl, who slipped it back to Luke who was waiting right behind them. At once, both big strikers shot off deep into the PSG half: Dog heading for Lama's left-hand post, and Carl for his right. Their sheer speed took the PSG defence by surprise.

That was part of the plan. Okpara and Co peeled away to give their closest attention to the Albion front-men. They all expected Luke to pump a high ball up to one of them. To the Studless Sensation, it looked like a blue-and-red sea parting. Then, suddenly, he had a clear view of the PSG goal – all of fifty yards away. And, just as Benny had predicted, Lama was out near the edge of his box. Why shouldn't he be? No one shoots from inside his own half – *do they*?

Luke, of course, did. Quickly he sized up the distance. He felt like one of those Six Nations rugby kickers who had taken countless shots at the posts on this very ground. But Luke wasn't aiming to send the ball sailing over the crossbar. He wanted his massive, blue-and-white-hooped rainbow of a shot to dip just under it. He took a deep breath, drew back his trusty right foot – then let fly.

Lama realized too late that he was being lobbed. Scuttling backwards, he tripped and fell in despair to the ground. All he could do was watch as the ball soared over him, then started to dip. With their hearts in their mouths, all the PSG fans watched too. But for Luke, it was sixth time unlucky. Unlike in training, his marksmanship was out by just a few millimetres. The ball scraped the underside of the crossbar and dropped down bang on the goal-line.

"*Ahhhhhhhhhhhhhhhhhhhhhh!*" sighed the PSG fans, sensing an escape.

But "*Go on , my son!*" yelled the far louder Albion faithful, when they saw Carl react fastest of all the players in the area. Lama scrambled to his feet and dived to try to scoop the bouncing ball away to safety. But Carl had other ideas. Launching himself through the air as if he'd just been smacked by a second pineapple, he met the ball full on his forehead and nodded it home.

As Luke's headmistress had said, goals pay the rent. And Albion had just put down a four-month deposit in advance. They'd done it! They'd pulled the first goal back! They were on their way!

But they didn't go mad celebrating. Rocky and his chorus did – but not the players. They'd agreed on this before. They had a job and a half to do that night. They had to keep plugging away until all *three* goals were in the net. So with their jaws set, they just trotted back for the restart – then got *really* stuck in.

The next half-hour or so wasn't tip-top footballing entertainment. PSG were rattled by that early goal, and clearly had no plans to concede another. But nor did they look much like scoring themselves. All they wanted to do was shut up shop, smother one Albion attack after another, and now and then lump the ball up to Madar, their lone striker, to relieve the pressure for a bit.

Albion had plenty of possession. They had a couple of goal-attempts too. Dog grazed the woodwork, Narris blasted a good chance wide from twelve yards. But, to be honest, they never really looked like going further in front. After his early booboo, Lama gobbled up everything that came his way. For Albion and their fans, it was frustrating. But as Benny tried to signal from the line, they just had to keep plugging away – in the end a goal was sure to come.

And it did. In the thirty-eighth minute. The only trouble was – PSG scored it.

No Albion player was to blame. The goal came from some pretty nifty PSG counter-attacking, not from a blue-and-white-hooped mistake. It started with Okocha winning a fifty-fifty ball with Chrissie close to halfway. At once he saw his fellow-Nigerian Okpara making a good overlapping run and fed him. Okpara hared down the right flank, and before anyone could close him down he hit a low cross to the near post. Madar flew in and scuffed his close-range shot. But still it rolled past the diving Madman's fingertips and into the net.

A phenomenal roar went up from the PSG fans. It hit Luke almost as hard as the goal itself. It seemed to affect the other Albion lads too for the rest of that half. Suddenly they seemed to go off the boil. Passes went astray, heads went down. Even Cool F nearly miskicked one of his clearances.

They struggled through to half-time without actually letting another goal in. But as they left the pitch with the songs of the jubilant *hoolicools* and Boulogne Boys ringing out, they knew that they still had it all to do.

Oddly, Benny didn't look too fed up as everyone trooped into the dressing-room. "For half an hour you were the best team by a mile," he told his tea-slurping heroes. "Or should I say 'by a kilometre' over here?"

Half the team frowned up at him. This really wasn't the time for terrible jokes. But at least it was better than watching tea-cups smashing into the wall.

"I agree with you, Benny," said Terry V. "We had 'em on the ropes for most of that half, but we didn't create enough chances. You're both doing great, Dog and Carl, but we're still looking a bit light up front."

"So d'you think we should bring another forward on?" panted Gaffer. "Casper or Keatsy or Darius? Give us a few more attacking options?"

"Maybe," said Benny, thoughtfully stroking his beard. "Maybe. But I reckon the eleven we've got out there now are the players to do the job. I can't fault any of you for effort, and apart from that last phase, you're all on song too."

"No changes, then?" said Dennis. "We just keep hitting them with what we've got?"

"Well, yes and no," said Benny, his eyes almost twinkling now. To look at him, you'd never have guessed that he was halfway through the most high-pressure game of his managerial career. Always full of surprises, old Benny. "I wanna stick with the same eleven, but try out a couple of *tactical* changes."

No one groaned, but a few eyeballs rolled. When it came to tactical thinking, Benny Webb was no Arsène Wenger. This was a man who, after all, sometimes put up a team-sheet with only ten names on it. He also had a habit of calling a flat back four a "flatpack four". And for years he'd thought the sweeper system was something to do with clearing the litter off Ash Acre's terraces.

"Steady on there, Boss," said Craig nervously. "If it ain't bust, don't fix it."

"But we've gotta pull out something extra in the second period, haven't we?" Benny asked with an eerily calm smile. "Unless we score three more goals we can kiss goodbye to this competition. And after comin' so far, as well. We've done amazingly just to *be* here. But I want more. I truly believe that our name is written on this cup. That we're gonna go all the way to Rome and win the thing! But unless we get those three goals now, all bets are off."

"So come on, Boss, let's hear it. What's your masterplan?" sighed Half-Fat. "Madman to play rush-goalie, is it? Or have we all got to play one-touch?"

Benny raised an eyebrow. He was *so* calm. Perhaps he'd poured the contents of his match-day hip-flask into his tea, but he didn't *look* drunk. "OK, listen up," he said. "Frederick, I think you're being wasted at the back. Apart from when they scored, they've hardly attacked us at all. So you've had precious little to do. In the second half, son, I want you plyin' your silky skills in the centre of midfield, right? Where *you* can do a bit of damage."

Frederick raised a finger to show that was cool with him.

"So we'll have a five-man midfield?" asked Narris. "Fred, Chrissie, Half-Fat, me and Luke? Won't we just get in each other's way?"

"I wouldn't wanna get in Narris's way," laughed Darius. "He'll kick anything."

"No worries there," Benny announced, "cos I'm shifting Luke up front. OK, Studless? We've gotta get you closer in to goal. It's all very well you shootin' from fifty yards. I'd like to see you wreakin' havoc up in their box now."

"Whatever you say, Boss," Luke replied. "Where d'you want me – wide on the right?"

"No, son. I want you to tuck in just behind Dog and Carl. Feed off their scraps, you know? Pick up their knock-downs. That sort of thing."

"Sounds good to me," nodded Carl. "We could use an extra body up front."

"How about you, Dog?" Benny asked. "You clear on all this, son?"

Dog sat up straighter and beamed broadly. "I am *exceedingly*—" he began.

"Yeah, right," said Benny, waving to show that he didn't need to hear the rest. "You'll cotton on soon enough. You're a smart old lad." Then he clapped his hands loudly and looked round the room. "You're *all* smart lads. You know what's at stake now. You know what I need from you. *Give* it to me!"

There was no shouting and whooping as the Albion squad filed back out for battle. This was way too serious now. Benny's words rang in all their ears. *You know what I need from you.* Luke knew it as well as any of the others.

It wasn't just Albion's UEFA Cup life that was at stake here. So was Big Ben's eleven-year-long life as Albion manager.

Jimbo's ghost had haunted that dressing-room right through half time. Where he was now was anyone's guess. But one thing was for sure: when he met Benny at noon tomorrow, he wasn't just going to ask him if he liked Britney Spears' new single or not. *This club's not big enough for both of us*, the Boy Wiz had growled. He was so furious, he would be looking for any excuse to sack the boss. But if Albion had just reached the UEFA Cup final, then no one and nothing on earth would be able to shift Benny from the manager's hot-seat.

As the crowd rose to welcome both teams back, Luke clenched his fists and gritted his teeth. Three goals. That's all they needed. Three little goals.

You could forget England, Harry and Saint George. This one was for Benny.

24

For Albion, the second half started no better than the first half had ended. PSG seemed to have overheard Benny's dressing-room chat. They went straight on to the attack – stretching Albion's new back three to the limit.

For more than ten minutes, Luke didn't get a touch in his new forward position. And Frederick, in midfield, could only watch as the ball sailed back and forth over his head. The Albion fans tried to lift the team by serenading the new formation:

> **"Jingle Bells, Jingle Bells,**
> **Jingle All The Way.**
> **Oh What Fun It Is To Play**
> **Three-Four-Three Away!"**

but it didn't feel like fun for Luke and the lads. Until just before the hour.

That was when Frederick at last got the ball at his feet, midway inside his own half. Yanovski, the Russian international, came snapping in but Frederick coolly side-stepped him before glancing upfield. Dog was the farthest forward, lurking near the edge of the box. At once Frederick sent a pinpoint pass to his chest. It was a real stunner. The ball never rose more than five feet from the ground, yet it curved through or round most of the PSG defence. Only Laspalles now stood between Dog and the goal as the Armenian Ace took the pass. Then, as the ball dropped, Dog pulled out something a bit special.

Like lightning he turned away to Laspalles' right, taking the defender with him. But in the same movement, he laid *back* the ball to the defender's left. Luke read it perfectly. Lama in goal was still watching Dog, as Albion's Terrier in Trainers surged through, picked up the lay-back with his first touch and then, with his second, passed the ball with laser accuracy into the net's far corner.

One-two! Albion had their noses in front again. Over on the touchline Benny didn't do his usual mad leaping and dancing. The rest of the Albion bench did. But Benny just stood there stroking his beard and nodding. *Tactics?* Who said Benny Webb couldn't do tactics?! He could do them on his head!

A monster chant of

"Benny Webb's Barmy Army!"

rang out as Luke trotted back to his own half – taking high-fives from the others but not getting carried away. Not yet. There were still two more goals to go. For Rocky and Co, however, the tie was already as good as won.

"Can We Play You Every Week?"
they boomed at the suddenly silenced Boulogne Boys. And then as the game got under way again,

"You're So French, It's Unbelievable!"
Luke smiled, then glanced at the clock. Half an hour left.

Over the next ten minutes, he looked at that clock maybe twenty times more. Not once, despite his deepest longings, did it start to run backwards. The minutes kept ticking away and, once again, a stalemate set in. Neither side seemed able to break out of the midfield dead-lock – which suited PSG perfectly. The longer this drab scuffling went on, the better they liked it. As things stood, they were four-three ahead over the two legs (although Carl probably thought it was more).

Albion badly needed another stroke of genius, like that set-up of Dog's for Luke's goal. And – miracle of miracles – in the seventy-second minute they got one.

This time Luke started it off. He'd dropped back a bit deeper to try to get more involved. Going for a fifty-fifty ball with Benarbia, he came out on top. Stumbling slightly from the challenge, he headed on into the PSG half, then nutmegged Cisse as he tried to close him down. Over on the left Chrissie was making a good run and yelling for the ball, but his marker was goalside of him. Luke looked right instead – and found Cool F.

It takes longer to describe what happened next than it took for Luke and Frederick to do it. Certainly no one in the PSG team was quick-witted enough to stop it. But, to be fair, the boys had been practising this move together for the best part of six years in the local park. There, they'd used a row of small trees as defenders. Now the dumbfounded PSG-ers stood just as rooted to the spot.

First off, Luke dug his foot under the ball and flicked it up on to the running Frederick's head. At once he set off, while Frederick headed it on without breaking step. So Luke was there, behind the first two defenders, to receive it back on his own head. But, instead of bringing it under control, he headed it straight to the still-flying Frederick again. And when *he* got it back, again he nodded it over into Luke's path – by which time five defenders had been left for dead.

Ping-pong-ping-pong! It mesmerized even the fans. But Rabesandratana – the last PSG player before Lama – at last wised up. As Luke reached the edge of the penalty area, Mr R began to backpedal at once, to intercept his next header back to Frederick. That gave Luke a clear sight of Lama's near post. And before you could even begin to say Rabesandratana, Luke leapt, flicked his neck and bulleted a header just inside that post and into the net. Oh *yes-s-s-s-s-s-s*!

One-three on the night! Four-four overall!

"One Lukey Green!!!"

Rocky's mob told the world.

"There's Only One Lukey Green!
One Lukey Greee-eeen!
He's The Best Ever Seee-eeen!"

Luke saluted them after touching fists with Frederick. They were singing his name so loudly, he was half-afraid his mum might hear – wherever she might be in the city. But he couldn't afford to worry about that. He'd brought the scores all-square. If no one else scored in the game's last stretch, that would mean extra-time. But Luke didn't fancy that. With only three at the back, Albion always ran the risk of shipping another goal. So they had to go for it. *He* had to go for it. For the out-and-out winner. For his hat-trick. For Benny.

But even Luke didn't think he'd get his chance so soon.

A blank-faced Madar nudged the kick-off to Okocha. The gifted Nigerian took a wild swing, intending to sweep a pass out wide to the left while pretending to look right. But the only person he tricked was himself. He lost his balance. And, falling, he sliced the ball straight to Luke, who was standing in his new forward position just on the centre-circle.

Now they say that lightning never strikes twice in the same place. And they're right. In one game of football, you can never do *exactly* the same thing twice.

But when Luke looked up, and saw Lama way off his line (and still screaming blue murder at his defenders for failing to stop the last strike), he repeated what he'd done at the start of the match. He took a huge, high, shot at goal.

And whereas the first time he ended up hitting the bar, *this* time the ball dipped at least two feet under it. Oh, oh, *oh*!

Until he watched the post-match video, Luke never saw it hit the net. By the time it did, he was already disappearing under a scrum of screaming team-mates. There was nothing to stop them from celebrating *now*. Albion were no longer playing catch-up. That stonking goal had put them five-four ahead on aggregate. With one piece of pure football genius, Luke had gone for it – and he'd got it! All of it! The out-and-out winner! His hat-trick! And surely now – beyond all doubt – he had made Benny's job safe as well!

PSG were finished. However hard they tried, however many subs they threw on, however much coach Bergeroo puffed and panted on the line, they could put in only one more worthwhile shot before the end. It wasn't a bad one, either – a volley on the turn from Yanovski that stretched Madman to the limit.

The diving keeper took the sting out of the shot, but the ball kept trickling goalwards after he fell to the ground. And it would have crossed the line, if one of the Albion players hadn't guessed in advance that this might happen. Already he was giving chase, then he slid in and hacked the ball away to safety. The name of this last-ditch hero? None other than the guy Benny had chosen over Jimbo: Narris-Narris-Narris *Phiz!* Had the big bad lad from Trinidad repaid his manager's faith in him now, or what?!

When the final whistle went, Luke sank to his knees, scarcely believing what had happened. And the first person to get to him was Mr Sheepskin himself – Benny "Tactics Turn Matches" Webb.

"Son," he boomed, pulling up Luke with one hand then handing him the match-ball with the other. "You get to keep this when you hit a hat-trick. You done me proud, Luke. You've done us all proud. This has made it all worthwhile! All the heartache and nonsense. I really..." He said more but Luke didn't hear it.

You don't tend to hear very much at all when an entire first-team squad, plus the coaching staff, plus several coachloads of insanely happy fans have jumped on top of you, kissing you so hard that you think they're sucking off your skin.

25

It was twenty minutes to midnight. The game had been over for hours. Yet *still* Luke was struggling to believe that it had all really happened.

It was as if at the final whistle he had gone into a kind of slow-motion dream. He felt as if his feet weren't quite touching the ground – in the dressing-room, in the showers, at the trendy restaurant afterwards as the champagne corks popped, and now as their huge party staggered down this wide Parisian street.

He could *hear* his joyful team-mates reliving every moment of the game and chanting "We're on our way to Rom-*a*!" over and over. He could *see* Benny Webb and Rocky Mitford dancing cheek-to-cheek along the edge of the pavement, with TAFKAG strumming away on his guitar behind them. He could *smell* the series of pies that Madman had smuggled across from England and was chomping through in celebration. He could *feel* Uschi's arm linked through his own. Yet none of these sensations seemed quite real to him.

In his heart, Luke had never quite believed that he would be at the game – let alone score three goals and be named Man of the Match. It had been such a struggle to get to Paris in the first place. And even after they'd got here, he had been sure his mum would foul it all up for him somehow. At no time until he stepped out on to that pitch had he dared to hope he would play. And then there were those other problems too. Getting the Dog in. Easing Jimbo out. All that planning and plotting. All for the sake of a single ninety-minute game. And now it had all paid off *big-time*! Albion were in the final of the UEFA Cup! Their dream had come true – yet still Luke couldn't seem to wake up.

"Still no word from our beloved chairman, then?" he heard Chrissie calling out. The Pickman was arm-in-arm with his own beloved Sara, an Albion bobble-hat planted on his hairless head and a big plastic pineapple tied round his neck.

"Nah!" Ruel called back, staring at his silent mobile phone and shrugging. "You'd think he would want to congratulate us, wouldn't you?"

"No chance!" laughed Terry V, who was trying to ride a plastic inflatable tandem with Darius Aldershot on the back. "He'll be throwing a right old wobbler. Mrs Plunkett will probably have to give him a good slap! But once he's calmed down, he'll be as chuffed as the rest of us. It *is* his club."

"Didn't someone say he flew straight back to England after he stormed out of the dressing-room?" asked Dennis.

"That's right," giggled Half-Fat. "Buzzed off in his own private jet, they said."

"I hope they were showing a good film on board," spluttered Madman through a huge mouthful of steak and onion and gravy and pastry. "Or he'll have started chucking his aeroplane food at the screen."

"Talking of chucking food," cried Craig, snatching the last bit of pie out of the keeper's hands, and hurling it into a waste-bin ten yards away. "You've got no idea how bad that stuff stinks!"

Without a care Madman delved into his jacket pocket, produced another pie and began to unwrap it. "Chicken and mushroom," he explained. "Low smell."

Luke strolled on in his stupor. With one hand he bounced his precious match ball on the pavement – just to make sure the pavement was still there.

"You bounce the ball and catch it so *smoothly*," Uschi purred in his ear. "Your talents are clearly not limited to the football pitch."

Luke smiled faintly, tried to disentangle his

arm from hers, found her grip too tight, then gave up. So far on this street she had asked him for a kiss seven times. Or maybe it was eight. He wasn't quite sure when Uschi had shown up after the game. It couldn't have been in the showers (could it?). But she'd definitely been there at the restaurant, along with several other unexpected faces. These included the entire ITV commentary team, who were still around.

There now, just in front of Luke and Uschi, an off-duty Gary Newbon was playing scissors-paper-stone with Casper Franks (and losing fairly heavily). While over to Luke's left, hands in pockets and looking even more relaxed than usual as he chatted with Cool F, was ... Mr Desmond Lynam.

Even in his dreamy state, Luke couldn't help thinking how weird that was. His mum would have given *anything* to be walking along so close to her hero. Her real hero – not a cardboard cut-out or a bit of film of him on TV. If only Luke could just call her up at the hotel and say, "Mum, he's here..."

Dream on! As a matter of fact, Luke and TAFKAG *had* tried to ring her earlier. They wanted to get her to OK it for Luke to stay with his dad that night. But there had been no reply from the room. Luke could only guess that she'd got over her food poisoning, and now at last she and Rodney were out on the town. Luke just hoped they weren't in any bars that showed football highlights.

Once again he bounced his match ball on the pavement. What a trophy this was! Terry had cleaned it up in the showers, then got all the squad to autograph it. (Well, all the ones who could write their own names.) When he got home, Luke would have to find somewhere good to hide it. A place where he could often go, then gaze at it, touch it, smell it, bring back all the fabulous memories.

"Oh, Luke," sighed Uschi, leaning closer into him. "The masterful way that you bounce that ball... It thrills me so... Oh, Luke, *Luke*, will you not kiss me...?"

Luke sighed too, pretending he hadn't heard. That was quite easy. Most of the squad had just gathered behind them and started chanting at deafening level:

"One Lukey Green!
There's Only One Lukey Green!
But His Mum Doesn't Kno-ow
Where Her Dear Lukey's Bee-een!!!!"

Luke smiled his vague smile. Then, as they came up to a major road junction, the squad went through the whole thing again, fluttering Albion scarves and streamers above his head. And round the corner came two figures. At once they looked familiar. A man and a woman, walking quite fast, heads down. But when they heard the dreadful din, they stopped suddenly and looked up.

The squad sang on. Uschi's grip on Luke's arm tightened. Luke froze. So did the couple standing no more than five paces away.

It was Luke's mum and Rodney!

Now Luke woke up. *Now* his previously blurry brain went into overdrive. This, he knew, did not look good. For here he was – not just holding a football, but being sung to in a very affectionate way by a dozen drunken professional footballers. This was it. The end.

Hide. *Hide!* He screamed inside himself. But there just wasn't anywhere for him to put himself. Nowhere to avoid his mum's frozen, bewildered gaze.

Or was there?

A thought fizzed through his head: *Distract her, distract her...* Clearly the same thought fizzed through Cool F's head, for he turned and nodded at his mate. A split second later, in their different ways, they both went into action.

Luke tossed his football back over his head, grabbed Uschi and swung her round into the nearest shop doorway. Once there, he answered all her prayers by wrapping his arms round her and giving her a kiss to send her on to a higher spiritual plane than even Mrs Plunkett knew about.

Meanwhile, Frederick tilted his head towards

Des Lynam and told him what he had to do.

Soccer's Mr Sensual didn't even blink. Straightening his tie, then stroking his moustache, he strolled over to where Luke's mum was standing. If her jaw had dropped when she saw Luke, it now pretty well dropped *off* when she saw Des.

But Mr L knew how to deal with starstruck ladies. After a wink at Rodney, the PSP (Pretty Smooth Presenter) simply bowed from the waist and offered Luke's mum his arm. Still gobsmacked, she took it, then let him turn her round and lead her away under the twinkling street lamps.

When Luke guessed the coast was clear, he pulled out of his clinch with the dazed but radiant Uschi. Everyone was staring at his mum and Des swanning off into the distance. Luke went over to Rodney, grinning at their great escape.

"There!" gasped Rod before giving his step-son a massive celebratory hug. "I knew that something really special was going to happen here. Something…"

"*Magical!*" chimed in everyone else as they joined in the hug.

Creatures

The Series With Bite!

Everyone loves animals. The birds in the trees. The dogs
running in the park. That cute little kitten.

But don't get too close. Not until you're sure.
Are they ordinary animals – or are they creatures?

1. Once I Caught a Fish Alive
Paul's special new fish is causing problems.
He wants to get rid of it, but the fish has other ideas...

2. If You Go Down to the Woods
Alex is having serious problems with the school play costumes.
Did that fur coat just move?

3. See How They Run
Jon's next-door neighbour is very weird. In fact,
Jon isn't sure that Frankie is completely human...

4. Who's Been Sitting in My Chair?
Rhoda's cat Opal seems to be terrified ... of a chair!
But then this chair belongs to a very strange cat...

Look out for these new creatures...

5. Atishoo! Atishoo! All Fall Down!
Chocky the mynah bird is a great school pet.
But now he's turning nasty. And you'd better do what he says...

6. Give a Dog a Bone
A statue of a faithful dog sounds really cute. But this
dog is faithful unto death. And beyond...

Creatures – you have been warned!

Paul Stewart

Football Mad
2-1 up in the inter-school cup final, captain Gary Connell finds the net ... at the wrong end! Now cup glory rests on a tricky replay...

Football Mad 2
Offside!
The inter-school cup is up for grabs again. But Craig won't be playing. He's been dropped – and he's not happy...

Football Mad 3
Hat-trick!
Could it be cup-final number three? Goalkeeper Danny is in trouble. New team coach Mr Carlton has really got it in for him...

HURRICANE HAMISH
Mark Jefferson

HURRICANE HAMISH
THE CALYPSO CRICKETER

Hurricane Hamish has always been a bit special –
ever since he was found washed up on a Caribbean
beach wrapped in an MCC towel. He's only twelve,
but he can bowl fast. Really fast. So fast he might
be about to play for the West Indies...

HURRICANE HAMISH
THE CRICKET WORLD CUP

Hurricane Hamish is back – and now he's in
England, determined to help the West Indies win the
Cricket World Cup. But England is so cold! The
grounds are so wet and slippery that Hurricane
can't even stay standing, let along bowl fast...

*"The ideal literary companion for this summer's
Carnival of Cricket – the World Cup."*
Lord MacLaurin, Chairman of the England and
Wales Cricket Board

*"Mark Jefferson has scored a real winner with
Hurricane Hamish ... this pacey romp of a book."*
Christina Hardyment, The Independent

"A novel which, like its hero, has pace and heart."
Nicolette Jones, The Sunday Times